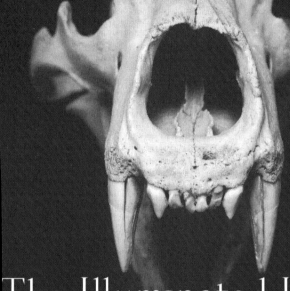

The Illuminated Heart

Thea van Diepen

THE UNDEAD FAIRY TALES COLLECTION

The Illuminated Heart

Heart

BY THEA VAN DIEPEN

Behold, the requisite legal material:

Cover design: Philip Pocock
Skull photo: Martin Wimmer
Author photo: Katie Leonardo
Illustrations: Thea van Diepen

ISBN: 978-0-9916993-5-3

This book is a work of fiction. Any resemblance these characters, settings, or events have to real people, places, or events is completely unintentional.

Otherwise, there would be some crazy uncanny valley *bleep* going on here.

To the one who led me through
the Valley of the Shadow of Death,
though I was afraid.

I am that no longer.

"Verið kyrrir og viðurkennið, að ég er Guð."
Sálmarnir 46:11a

"Be still and know that I am God."
Psalm 46:10a (NIV)

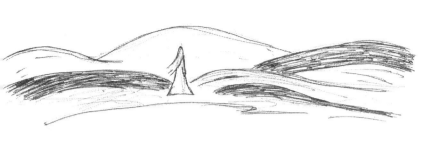

Part One
God has left me

CHAPTER ONE:
Funeral

The bearers lowered my baby brother feet first through the grave-door and I felt nothing. Not yet. Around me, my family and members of our village murmured prayers while they wept. A wind started, spreading cold like knives, but I only wrapped my shawl tighter around me. Winter edged the air; prophesied by the wind and sky.

As the bearers settled my brother into his barrow, I tried not to think of how small he was. There didn't need to be so many bearers, but they were all my father's closest friends, and they wanted to do honour to him at the loss of his only son.

They withdrew out from the barrow's entrance, picked up their tools, and began bricking up the doorway. Auðun, my father's gentle younger brother, was having a hard time keeping his hands steady, and left some of the bricks crooked. The others silently straightened these when they noticed them. At one point, he stumbled and kicked a small hole in their work, his face wet with silent tears. My father went to him, but Auðun shook him off and replaced the bricks.

When the grave-door had been sealed, Símon, the priest, sang a hymn. He had spoken against my father's plans for a barrow, denouncing it as a pagan tradition, but my father had wanted his son to be buried like a Viking hero, treated like a king of Iceland. Seeing that my father's only motivation was his love for his son, Símon had relented, so long as the entrance to the barrow was closed against any evil that might gain power through such a burial.

The hymn fell on me like a slow, pounding rain. I only wanted to be out from under its touch.

Its strains slowed to a trickle, then stopped. Our gathering disbanded and I followed my weepy family home.

After I helped my mother and sisters make dinner, I ate in attentive silence, though my mind had strayed to the hills outside our farm.

While washing up, Mother noticed my restlessness.

"Go on," she said. "Your sisters and I can manage the rest."

I ran from the house, past my father's fields, up and up until I had crested the hill at the edge of the farm and the land spread out before me, wide and hard and empty. The wind arose, tugging my hair away from the sun's lingering warmth, and I followed it down the embankment to the place where rock met the curve of the river. Running my hand over the familiar stone wall, I picked my way along the narrow shore, still following the breeze despite its loss of strength behind this shield. I reached a trail of stepping stones, crossed the river, and climbed up the other side.

The sky spread over the hills, raked by thin, grey clouds that seemed to reach like claws from the distant mountains, carved of light and darkness in the face of the setting sun.

"Where were you!" I screamed, the words scraping the air, becoming clouds of their own. "Where were you when my father prayed and prayed for a healthy son? Where were you when my brother was born sick? *Where were you?* How can you say that you love your children when you would do this? When you would allow this?" I spit in God's face, daring him to answer. To speak, like he did to the prophets, like he must have to Jesús when he prayed so earnestly that his death pass him by and blood ran from his brow like sweat.

'Hearing another means ceasing to speak,' my grandmother used to say, so I held back my words and let the silence fill the sky like a tangible thing, thick and heavy. My spirit raged, but I held to as much stillness as I could, giving a space for the words I craved. Stiff and straight as an aspen, I strained to listen until my back cried out for release.

All I heard was a murmuring, like a wheel turning round and round, speaking nothing more than nonsense, nothing more than garbled noise through water. I laughed, pebbles falling from the scree.

"So, you would leave me here, then? You're the one who promises good things; the one who says he will protect and prosper his children. Have you forgotten that? No, you gave my mother and father a child of prayer and, when death took him, you did nothing. Are you so different from us that you have no heart, that you would not even shed a tear while we ache with loss? I have been very wrong, if this is so." Thoughts of how my parents and Father Símon would speak of God and his love rose in my mind like a soft fragrance, shy in the face of the fire within me.

I squatted on the grass, letting my back relax for a moment before I turned away from the mountains and sat down.

"You have to give my father another son. I know Mother is getting too old to have children, but you gave Sara and Abraham a child when she was ninety-nine and he was a hundred. You gave them Ísak. You can give me a brother." My feet dangled down the escarpment, heels brushing against the brittle stone and stray clumps of grass. I pulled out a few green blades and broke them into pieces as tears pushed against my eyes. "Finally, I thought, finally there'd be a boy in the house and we'd be complete. Someone my sisters and I could dote on, who Father could take out into the fields and teach how to be a man. Someone Mother could kiss and call her sweet boy. It didn't even matter that he was sick for so long. He'd get better; he was from you. But he didn't." I threw the bits of grass down into the river, but they hit a jutting rock first and stuck there. The tears slid down my cheeks and I didn't try to stop them. Wind teased at the bits of grass, shifting them as I stared with a mind blank and a heart turning like the handle on a well. I couldn't tell if the water was coming or going.

"Fine. Say nothing, but at least show me a sign." My spirit grew firm. "You owe me that much, at least, while I wait for more. In a moment, I will stand and turn back towards the mountains. Show me something that will tell me what I need to hear." I inhaled, tense.

He wouldn't show me anything.

No, I couldn't accept that. He had made the fleece wet when Gídeon had asked, and made it dry again when he had called for proof that God was with him. I had asked for nothing so specific;

12

nothing so impossible. God would come. He had to come.

Taking another breath, I stood, brushed the dust from my skirt, and turned around.

At first, I could see nothing, but I wasn't willing to let God get away so easily, so I looked harder. Out among the hills, coming across them at a great speed, was a white animal. It was just a sheep, certainly, but, as it came closer, I began to realize that I was watching the approach of a bear. A polar bear, savage and wild, and I was most definitely its target.

God, what kind of sign *was* this?

I hiked up my skirt and ran, ran, ran. The bear was far enough away that I could escape it, or at least its sight, and get to safety.

The river should slow it down, I thought as I raced across the stepping stones and back along the bank. *It would have to ford the waters. They aren't as strong as in spring, but the flow should still be enough. It should be.*

Returning to the hill above my family's farm, my heart sped at the sight of my house, and the thought that I had not escaped danger, that I was bringing it home. But looking back would slow me down. I could do nothing more than listen while I raced past the fields, listen with wide ears for the sound of bear footfalls hiding in the voice of the wind.

There! There! My hands fumbled at the door, before I crashed through and cried out for my father. Then, with the house at my back and the sound of my father running to me, I searched the hill for the bear.

Gone.

"Dagný, what's wrong? What is it?" My father stood behind

me, following my gaze. But he saw what I did: the sky and the land, the place they touched, and nothing more. "What's wrong?"

It had been a sign of hostility. A sign of anger. A sign that God wanted nothing to do with me.

My heart broke, finally, and my father caught my limp body before I fell to my knees with weeping. He held me close and stroked my hair, trying to soothe me with a shaking voice and cracked words that I didn't hear.

Kaj Arasson, I will miss you.

CHAPTER TWO:
In My Father's House

Three weeks after the funeral, our ram went mad and killed several of our sheep before we could stop him. As my father and I held him, his rage finally calm, he shuddered and died. The next day, my eldest sister, Eir, found the rest of the sheep dead, their stomachs torn open and their guts arranged around their bodies in a grotesque artistry. She ran into the house, screaming, and it took my mother and me a very long time to calm her. Father went out to the pasture to clean up the remains without a word. It took him most of the day, so Mother sent us out in turns to do what we could of his usual responsibilities. When he came inside for supper, he kissed her and thanked us before collapsing into his chair.

Despite his quick work, by noon the next day, the entire village knew what had happened on our farm. Father Símon came to our house that evening to inform us of the rumours our friends and family had been spreading, and asked us if any were true.

"They say a legion of demons possessed your sheep and made them kill each other."

My father had no choice but to explain to the priest what had happened, his voice soothing as he blamed it on nothing more than a disease of madness whose spread he had stopped. It would not pass to the rest of the village.

I was washing clothes as Father Símon voiced concerns. Seeing movement out of the corner of my eye, I turned my attention to what had been the sheep pasture. In it stood a child, its skin a dark blue that had turned nearly to black. As it approached the house, I recognized it. It moved with the lithe purpose of a predator and its eyes held years its body could not possibly have seen, but I recognized it. The clothes slipped from my hands, splashing me with water I didn't feel, my stomach wrung so tight I could barely keep it from emptying.

It was Kaj —my brother, his corpse returned to life. I screamed and fell back, arms instinctively outstretched as if to ward off evil. My father and the priest rushed to me, but my throat had sealed itself and I could only point at the apparition. They both crossed themselves when they saw him.

He stopped at the edge of the pasture. Smiled.

"Did you like my gift, father?" Gone was the lisp of childhood, the warmth of love. All that remained was the cold and the dark.

My father shuddered.

The corpse gave him a sour look. "Then I shall have to give you more." He sped back across the field and out of sight, the three of us watching. I tried to calm my ragged breathing. But the hand that had wrapped itself around my heart had grabbed hold of my lungs as well.

"I shouldn't have allowed that pagan burial," said Father

Símon, his voice shaking. He crossed himself again and left my father and me to understand what we had just seen.

Oh, God. My brother, I thought. *My Kaj.* A draugur.

Two weeks later, our goats succumbed to the same madness as the sheep. Rumours flew around the village that we had been cursed because of the barrow Kaj had been buried in, that we held some secret sin in our family and that the draugur had appeared to punish us, that Father had turned to paganism and had called up his son from the dead only to find a monster had come instead. People avoided us in church, refused to speak to us more than necessary. Even our relatives kept themselves separate, and no longer invited us to their homes for any reason. No one came to our house, not when invited, not even for business. Walking through the streets made me feel filthy with stares.

At the end of those weeks, late in the evening, someone knocked on the door. My father stood to answer it.

"What if it's..." Mother stared at him, her expression strained. Father shook his head and motioned that we stay back. He opened the door.

"Ari, I'm so sorry." Auðun fell at my father's feet, his entire body shaking with sobs.

"What are you talking about? Get up, man." But, no matter how my father tried, Auðun would not rise, would not stop crying.

"It's because of me your son has come back to haunt you. When I fixed that hole in the barrow door, I was embarrassed and wanted only to be done, so I only made it look like I'd put enough mortar between the bricks. It would have been easy for a draugur

17

to find the cracks and tear them open. I did this to you!" Father knelt down and held his brother for a long time. Finally, he calmed and they both stood again.

"You have done nothing to me. I forgive you."

No. I couldn't stand to listen, so I fled to the cow pasture. My own uncle had been the one to cause this. He hadn't done it on purpose, that much would be clear to anyone who had seen him at the funeral, to anyone who had seen him with my father. I wanted to hate him.

"And so, the ice princess adds another wall to her castle," said a sibilant voice, soft with mockery. The draugur that my brother had become sat, legs dangling, on the fence. His face, swollen with death, still carried an unsettling resemblance to the little boy I held in my heart, but the eyes were cold with calculation. His skin, more blue than black in the sunlight, glistened as if it were coated unevenly with oil. I breathed carefully, trying to slow my heart.

"Are you here to kill me?"

"I could, couldn't I?" He cocked his head to one side, and some of his hair fell away, hanging like dead snakes. I swallowed, my mouth gone dry and my tongue stuck to my throat.

The draugur gave a short bark of a laugh. "Oh, but you will be the first to leave the world of the living. Mother and Father will outlive this, as will all our sisters, but you... I will wait a while yet." Draugar are said to know the future, and this prophesy pierced my heart with winter steel.

"Liar. I will see your end."

"Oh, certainly. But not with those eyes." I shut out the sight of him and clenched my skirt, as if that would make him vanish in reality. Make *it* vanish. It didn't.

As we settled into bed that night, the draugur climbed up onto the roof. We could hear its shoes scrape against the walls, its weight on the turf above. For a moment, silence fell, and I lay rigid under my blankets. We all did, rigid and barely breathing as we waited to find out what it would do. I thought it would break through and fall upon us, or that it would destroy the house and leave us to the elements. Instead, it started beating on the roof, a steady drumming that shook the turf without damaging it. Relieved, I turned over and tried to sleep.

The pounding continued the entire night, incessantly, rhythmically. We would nearly become used to the pattern, then it would change and we would all sit straight up in our beds, the hairs on our necks standing on end.

I couldn't understand why it didn't just tear down the house and kill us. Why would it toy with us like this? But, with every two-beat, I could hear my name.

Dag - ný.

Dag - ný.

Dag - ný.

The first to leave the world of the living.

God, you heard what it said. If you truly cared about my family, you would make it kill me.

You don't really want that, surely?

It didn't matter what I wanted. God wouldn't give it to me. Auðun may have weakened that door, but God could have stopped this terror from coming through. Didn't he work out all things for good for those that love him? Did we not love him?

Oh, my child, you do not see…

"Oh, of course not. Your ways are higher than mine," I muttered, then lay back in bed and covered my head with my pillow to keep out the sound of the blows and tried to sleep.

For weeks, this continued, thinning our tempers and carving youth from our faces. We wanted to stop the menace, but what could we do? Draugar have strength and cunning beyond that of the living. They can cause a person to go mad, curse them, bring the wind and rain against them. We prayed, of course, but anything more was beyond our power. My mother began to look sick with exhaustion. Father took to spending all his time out in the fields and tending the animals, no matter whether they truly needed it. My sisters and I got into so many arguments over silly things that I stopped speaking to anyone. It allowed me some energy to avoid falling asleep in the middle of the day, and the tongue-lashing from my mother I would have to endure after.

Our entire crop of rye fell prey to some kind of blight my father had never encountered before. It left the grain hollow, and the plants withered and useless. Before long, my father would go out to his ruined fields, only to sit, unmoving, with the dust blowing around him in the cold wind.

The vegetables succumbed to another disease. I cut open a potato one day only to find that it had turned to liquid on the inside, and the white slime spilled onto my hands and the table. My stomach turned over, and I ran outside to vomit. Even after emptying myself, I couldn't stop retching; my insides twisted into more and more unnatural positions with every spasm.

Similar misfortunes started passing to the rest of the village and, one by one, all of our neighbours, friends, and relatives left. Even Auðun, though he and Father spent nearly half a day together before he did. Soon, we were the only people who remained in the entire town, cut off by the monster. That. Monster.

What had we done to deserve this?

The day the horse died, a storm blew in which darkened the sky such that it seemed the entire world had turned black. The draugur stayed out of his barrow at all times, and we stayed in the house with the door locked and barricaded in case it might try to come inside.

"Father, this can't go on," said Eir that day at supper. "We have to leave, or we'll starve."

"Where would we go?" Father asked.

"The farm is ruined. It doesn't matter where we go, so long as it isn't here. With… that *thing.*" She stared at him with wide eyes, her jaw clenched. Father sighed and stirred his soup while the rest of us waited, motionless, for his decision. The draugur who had been my brother crashed violently against the roof, causing bits of turf to fall onto the table.

"We will not leave."

Protestations rose up all around the table, but I remained silent, as did Mother. I raised my eyebrows at her, as she was always the last to hold from speech. She indicated my father's face. His lips were thin, set, and his eyes remained on his soup. She was right. Sometime since the draugs arrival, without our noticing, he had set his mind on this matter. He wouldn't change

21

it, no matter how loud anyone spoke against him.

"We may be lapping death up from a shell right now, but we have to trust God to show us a way through it. He will take care of us; show us what we need to do."

I snorted. "That's why Father Símon was the first to leave, no doubt."

The room grew utterly silent. Even the draugur had stopped its pounding. I bit my tongue —those words had only been meant for the confines of my own mind.

"We're not leaving," said my father, his voice low. "And that's all we will say on the matter."

Outside, the draugur began to laugh, the pitch rising from bass through to soprano and then up and up until we could no longer hear it.

CHAPTER THREE:
An Invitation

Somehow, we survived the month, but winter had filled the air and wind and, with no harvest, no animals, and no one to rely on for help, I knew we wouldn't be able to last. Mother and Eir had rationed out all of our remaining food, stretching it as much as possible and, while they said we would be fine, they wouldn't give us a count of anything.

Night had taken up residence, and we had undressed for bed to the sound of the draugur climbing the house when there came a roar. It blasted through the house, this wild voice of some great beast, and left in its wake an uncanny silence. I clenched my teeth and stood, ears straining for any other evidence of this animal so that I could ascertain how dangerous it was. The only thing I heard was the draugur hurriedly climbing back down the house and its feet against dirt as it ran away. And then, a soft knocking at the door.

My heart shuddered.

Someone moaned inside the house, stopping only when Father spoke sharply to them. He approached the door, the rest of us following. We stared at it with thin faces, and my father glanced back at my mother, his face lined with the fear we all felt crouching in our bones. The thing outside knocked again. Mother nodded, and my father opened the door.

The moon hung in the sky, ripe with light, and, shining beneath it, was a polar bear. It nodded at my father.

"Good evening."

Openmouthed, my father nodded back.

"The same to you." The words came out flat. It sounded inadequate against the enormity of the situation. I hardly knew how I would have reacted, in his place.

The polar bear turned its gaze to the rest of us, surveying the inside of our house as it did. When it came to me, its eyes lit up. I tilted my face away, wanting to hide, but couldn't keep from looking back at it. It huffed, then addressed my father again.

"Will you give me your youngest daughter? If you will, I'll make you as rich as you are now poor." My mother placed her hands on my shoulders, but didn't speak. I could barely breathe, caught by the memory of how the polar bear might know me.

"M-may I speak with her first?" said my father. The bear stepped back.

"Certainly."

My father closed the door. He leaned against it, exhaling. Mother let go of my shoulders and started herding my sisters away.

"Elka—"

"I want nothing to do with it," she said to Father, her back to him.

He opened his mouth.

"Nothing."

Once the bedroom door closed, my father sighed.

I crossed my arms and stared at the floor.

"You'll be safe with him. I can't say why, but I know you won't be harmed, and that he'll keep his word." My lips twisted into a grimace of disbelief. Father's legs shook. He sat down. "I think this is the help God promised."

Help. Certainly. Anything with even a hint of kindness would seem like God's help to my father, given the circumstances. I knew better.

"No." I spoke hoarsely. It had been so long since I'd said anything that my throat and mouth had almost forgotten how to form sound.

"Dagný, he can make this menace go away. He can bring us our life again, a better one, even. Go with him."

"No." The word came clearer this time. The bear knocked on the door again. Before my father could stand, I opened it. The bear stood, huge in the doorway, its eyes only on me.

"I cannot stay here any longer. Have you decided?"

"Why?" I wanted to say more, to ask why it would want to take me away from my family, why me and not one of my sisters. I wanted to ask why it had chased me after the funeral. I wanted to ask why God had sent it —if God had sent it. But I could only manage the one word and hope it understood. Father didn't.

"Dagný— " He shook his head and tried to open the door further to stand in front of me. I didn't let him. Staring straight into the eyes of the bear, I didn't let him. The bear's eyes widened.

"I saw you in the hills and you were afraid. And I was not."

My nostrils flared, and I clenched my jaw.

25

"Come back in a week." I shut the door.

Father pushed past me and swung it open, but the bear was gone. Only the white moon hung in the sky and darkened the stars with its splendour.

"Will you go with him then?" asked my father.

"No."

"Then why would you tell him to return?" I stared at him, trying to come up with a reason that would suit him. Nothing came.

I went back to bed.

For the next week, my father and sisters pestered me about the bear. Would I go with it? Did I really want it to come back? What would I do or say once it had? While I changed my words each time, I only did so to keep them from saying any more, to keep them thinking that I hadn't settled on anything. My answers were always the same in my mind: No, yes, I don't know. They wouldn't like those answers. Wouldn't understand them. I hardly did myself. At nights, I would cry out to God in my mind, calling for him to deliver us; to make the draugur kill me so that my family could see an end to their suffering, and so I could see an end to the weight the bear had put on me. He never answered.

"You can't keep wearing the coat on both shoulders, Dagný," said my father the day before the bear's expected return. I shrugged, and continued to stir the soup, made of little more than water and a few carrots. He shook his head. "You have to think of the good of the entire family. How long do you think we'll be able to live on soup as thin as that? If we don't accept the bear's offer, someone is going to die before this winter ends. Or all of us." My eyes closed involuntarily, and I shivered. The draugs words out at the sheep pasture echoed through my mind with painful remembrance.

A strange thought hit me: What if the draugur had prophesied my end not at its hands, but at the teeth and claws of a bear? What if the riches the bear promised would come because of its vanquishing the draugur with my blood? Father was so certain that the polar bear brought with it the saving power of God. It could be. It could have been that saving power back when I had run from it. It could be that running from it had caused all this trouble, and that running towards it would end it. All I needed to do was learn the future before it happened.

"I'll know my decision when it arrives, don't worry Pabbi. Everything will be fine."

He pressed his lips together.

"Are you sure?" I shrugged, and continued to wash the dishes.

I slipped away the next day as the sun had begun to caress the sky, and headed out to my brother's barrow. My weakened body could barely take me there, so I had to stop to rest. White clouds painted the blue above me, their touch soft with pearls.

God, help me, I thought.

He murmured, and I tried to filter words from him, but none made any sense. Tears pricked my eyelids. *I don't want to do this, but what other choice do I have? You won't speak to me, and I need answers. What else do you expect? I can't sit and do nothing.* More murmuring. More. Hateful. Murmuring. I got up and continued.

As I approached the mound, I could see the draugur sitting

27

in front of the grave-door with that terrible hole in the bricks, picking dirt out from under its fingernails.

"Come to disturb the dead, I see," it said without looking at me.

"You seem to have done that well enough yourself," I replied, my voice hoarse from exertion. My muscles ached, and the one thing I wanted the most at that moment was to sit down, but I refused to be companionable with that creature. I had come for information; nothing more. It looked up sideways, squinting.

"You haven't given up, have you? The game hasn't even begun to get interesting." I took a breath. Let it out. The creature shrugged and turned its attention back down.

You have one more chance, I told God.

Will anything I say make any difference? I wanted to weep and shout at him. Yes, yes, it would make a difference! He would tell me how he'd already fixed this; how he'd taken away the need to consort with the undead or leave my family. He would take over, and I wouldn't have to try anymore. I could just let it all go.

His voice dissolved again to the turning wheel.

"I'm getting bored. Shall I find us something to do, or will you eventually come to your point?" The draugur shifted position.

God?

Nothing.

I let go of my skirt and inhaled.

"You can tell the future. What will happen if I go with the bear?" I clenched my skirt with as much strength as I had left in my hands. The draugur snorted.

"Oh, it's not a matter of if," it said, continuing to clean its nails. "You *will* go, and you'll bring destruction down on him."

So it was. So it would be.

Evening came, ushered in with tense silence. We didn't undress for bed, and the draugur didn't climb onto the roof. I sat in a corner, away from the rest of my family. No matter how much they tried to keep me company or get me to talk, I only withdrew from their presence, hoping that they would leave me to what I knew I had to do for them. They couldn't know; I refused to tell them. All I could see was how thin they all were, and how weak. All I could think of was how… how…

From the door came a knock. Father went to answer it, but I stood, pushed him gently to the side, and opened it. The bear stared at me with its black eyes.

"I will go with you."

CHAPTER FOUR:
Not Afraid

The polar bear carried me on its back towards the mountains.

Its fur was coarser than I had expected, with a soft layer beneath that kept my legs and hands as warm as the summer sun. I accepted this as a small comfort for me as I went to my fate, and buried as much of myself in it as I could.

We came to a halt at the foot of one of the larger mountains, brooding in the darkness. A small breeze picked up, blowing my hair haphazardly around my face. I started to dismount, but the bear growled. It was staring at the sky, so I followed its gaze. Above the mountains, with shy tendrils, the northern lights had begun to grace the black. They hung for a moment, shimmering. Then, in a plunge of confidence, they filled the sky, streaming outward in a glorious green. They danced above the mountain peaks, their movement profound, as if they held all the mysteries of creation. The bear and I watched in silence, as if time had stopped and all that existed was this moment and the illuminated sky. When the lights had faded back into the north, the bear sighed like nothing could be added to its joy. I didn't dare let myself feel anything, for fear it might overwhelm me.

"Are you afraid?" the bear asked, turning its head so that it could see me out of one eye.

No, I wasn't.

The bear huffed and continued on its winding way through the mountains, its gait so gentle that it lulled me to sleep. I entered almost at once into bizarre, vivid dreams that I couldn't make any sense of.

Red pulsed in the background as black and green battled over a white animal. I tripped into an ocean, crying out as I sunk deeper and deeper, but the only response I got was the fur that began growing all over my body. It itched and I pulled it out, wounding myself in the process. I screamed. The white animal broke free from the colours above and plunged into the water, having somehow transformed into a star. It reached to me with a hand of light, and I reached back. Before we could touch, I hit rock and then there was nothing.

Stars danced across my vision, then a gentle washing of pink and orange. The bear's rolling gait and the feel of its muscles beneath me came into my awareness like a slow pour of water.

I opened my eyes to see the sky lit up and clear of clouds. My arms and legs were still warm beneath the polar bear's fur, but my back felt as if it had been turned to ice. I shivered.

"We will arrive soon," said the bear, its voice deep and rough. I nodded, forgetting that it couldn't see me, and then tried to find out where it had taken me.

Waves pounded against the curve of stone, worn as it was from the sea, and whispered as they slid along the gravel of the shore. The spray blew out from above the rocks and spattered my face with salt. The bear walked along the place where the shore met the mountains, heading towards a cliff that jutted out like a wall into the ocean. I yawned and stretched as well as I could, my mind still fuzzy from sleep.

After so many nights of so little peace and waking more tired than I had been when I'd gone to bed, I could hardly believe how rested I felt. My stomach growled for a moment before retreating back to its place of hollowness.

Soon, I told it, *Soon you won't have to worry about that any more.*

It seemed almost cruel that I had been given a night like that before my end. At the same time, it comforted me that God would grant me a measure of goodness on this earth before I left it. Surely this meant that he cared at least a little about my needs. I murmured something that was unintelligible even to me, but I knew I was thanking him for his kindness, and I think he knew as well.

The polar bear reached the cliff and stopped. It sniffed, snorted, then reached out with a forepaw and knocked on the stone. With a grinding, the cliff opened to reveal a gate. It opened and the polar bear entered. I had to press as flat as possible against its back to fit through the opening, and the bear's fur tickled my face.

"You may dismount." Its words echoed in what sounded like a vast room. I kept my focus only on the bear. This had gone on long enough.

I slid off the bear's back, wincing at the pain in my legs that came from sitting for so long.

The bear's eyes softened. "I'm sorry."

"It's fine." The executioner asking forgiveness for its victim's discomfort? It didn't matter. We had arrived; my time had ended. I took a deep breath to release the clenching in my stomach. I didn't want to die.

"Don't you like my castle?"

"Does it matter?"

The bear huffed and looked at its forepaws. I sighed. "We should do what we're here for."

"What?"

Its head shot up, eyes wide.

"I know that the saving of my family requires my death. I understand that now, though I didn't the first time you saw me."

"Killing you is the very last thing I would ever do," said the bear quietly. Its bulk sagged, its ears drooped, and its eyes glistened with tears that fell like small stars to the cold stone floor. I watched, my chest light and back straight, as the bear shook its head, restraining the shuddering in its sides. Something broke within it, and the sobs came through, neither the howls of an animal nor the weeping of a man, but something far stranger. Beautiful, even. "I have been searching for so long…"

"You mean to keep me alive?"

"Of course!"

"But the draugur prophesied. It said—"

The polar bear's roar filled the room, a storm of sound, wiping out any trace of the end of my sentence.

"It lied."

I opened my mouth to contradict.

"No, say no more. You are safe. Your family is safe. There is nothing for you to fear, especially not the words of a monster like that." It went to a small table next to the gate, on which stood a small silver bell, which it then picked up and handed to me.

"I don't understand," I said, holding the thing with both hands.

The bear sighed, a small wind in an empty cavern.

"Ring it, and you will receive anything you need. I may have promised wealth to your family in exchange for your presence, but I would never mistreat you because of that. You may see me as nothing more than a wild animal. If that is so, then you are blind." With that, it turned and started to lumber away.

The draugur had told me that I would go with the bear, so I did. Was that true prophesy? It had little case to be. If it was, then were the rest of its words also true, or would it have lied to drive me to my end? I could take that chance.

"You can talk," I said. The bear stopped. "You can talk, and you came when I called for a sign from God. And you came when my family was about to die, offering them blessing. I would never see you as a mere beast, no matter what you looked like." I could see its entire body relax at my words. It felt empty, just to say those. The walls around me seemed to lean in, asking for the part that would complete my peace offering. I scrambled.

Ask his name.

That has nothing to do with this, God. I need to tell him something more, something that will turn him around and, and…

What?

I don't know. Something important.

Ask his name. Lord of Creation, stubborn as a mule. Rolling

34

my eyes at him, I steeled myself for the disapproval of one of the most dangerous creatures I'd ever met.

"What's your name?"

The polar bear glanced back at me, holding my gaze longer than was comfortable. I held it, feeling that confidence suited its expectations the best. It nodded, then continued on its way.

"I am called Finnr. Please, ring for whatever you need. I will return soon." Then it left through a door on the far end of the room.

With the bear gone, I finally let myself see the splendour I stood in. The walls hung with ornate, abstract artwork, framed with gold and silver. The room, clearly an entrance to a grand palace, held a staircase with steps of white stone veined with black, walled by railings of dark wood polished to shine in the light of a thousand-candled chandelier. There were no windows.

It suddenly occured to me that I had accepted the help of a talking polar bear who promised to magically rescue my family from the ravages of a draugur, and who had then taken me to a castle hidden in a cliff by an ocean I had never before set eyes on. That I was living a sequence of impossibilities.

What power had made this possible? Was this the answer to prayer, or something darker than what I had left because it appeared to be light?

I should have been feeling something, anything, and my heart did try to burst open, but I wrapped everything close to me so it couldn't get away. I didn't know what it was that wanted expression, and I didn't want to know. Finnr... Finnr truly wanted to help. But I knew I'd die regardless.

A draft slid its fingers through my clothes and across my skin, causing me to pull my shawl tighter around me with one hand. The other held the silver bell that Finnr had given me. After all this winter, the only thing I could think to desire was warmth.

I rang the bell.

Part Two
At the bear's mercy

CHAPTER FIVE:
Good Riddance

For days, I did nothing but sleep, eat, and sit wrapped in blankets so warm that I could almost feel myself melting from the heat. The bell brought me whatever I wanted, both ordinary Icelandic fare and exotic food and drink, delicacies I had only heard of from travellers passing through the village, and it took me to wherever I wished, so long as I remained inside the castle. I spent nearly all my time in front of a fireplace, preferring to sleep there rather than in a bedroom. Finnr would come to visit and tried often to start conversation, only to leave after too much quiet. He growled sometimes as he did, deep in his throat. Part of me felt guilty for my silence and yet, after so long with so little speech, I couldn't think of anything to say. And what *would* one say to a polar bear? What kinds of things would you discuss with it? Yes, I knew Finnr to be a person, in a sense, but, person or not, we were still two very different creatures with little in common.

It didn't matter. My body's needs had drawn to the forefront now that they could be properly met the first time since winter had begun. Cold radiated out from my core, entwined with exhaustion. The blankets and the food and the fire served as my attempt to re-ignite the flame within me, the one that had been taken by the draugur. As much as they soothed the surface, they could never penetrate through to my true need.

One evening, Finnr and I sat on the floor in front of the fireplace, me curled up next to him beneath a thick wool blanket. I expected the time to continue as all the others had, lost without words, so it surprised me when I realized that I finally had something to say. Where it had come from, I couldn't tell, but there it was, shyly pressing at my lips to be released.

"My name is Dagný," I said. Finnr raised his head, ears pricked up and eyes wide. "I don't think I told you that yet."

"I didn't mind." He sighed, putting his head back down. He looked happier, somehow. It gave me the courage to let another sentence escape through my mouth, a question this time.

"What were you doing out there in the hills before we first saw each other?" Both Finnr and I stared into the flames, watching the dancers of light as they leapt and tried to fly. A log fell to the side in a shower of sparks, as if freeing spirits of the tree who had been trapped when the axe had brought it crashing down. One of the sparks landed by the blanket, glowed for a moment, and then went out with a sigh.

"Waiting." Finnr shook his head to dislodge an ember from his nose, then put it out with his paw.

"For what? Me?"

"That's not the right word." Finnr scratched under his ear with one paw, intent on the flames that hissed and spat from the wood. "I... waited. I held calm in my heart and the expectation of good, only good. I reflected in my heart on that good, pondered it and gave it form in my imagination, made it become

40

reality inside until it was so real that outside reflected it back to me. I asked God for the inspiration I sought. It became my sight."

"What did you see?"

"You."

I wrapped the blanket more tightly around me, trying to understand what Finnr had just described. Was there a word for it? What was it?

"So... you prayed for me, and God brought me to you, is that how you saw it?" The fire reached a pocket of sap in the wood and started a tantrum. I reached out of the blanket, picked up the poker and shifted the logs until they settled down. "Why were you looking for me?"

Finnr snorted and moved so that I couldn't see his eyes.

"I can't say. But pray is a good word. I wanted to know God's will, and to live it. It's a good word for what I did."

We let the dance of light and heat mesmerize us for a while.

"Dagný?" Finnr rolled over, eyes gazing into mine.

"What?"

"Why do you still sit and sleep here with that blanket wrapped around you? Is the castle too cold?"

"No, the castle's fine." I laughed, touched by his concern. "I just can't seem to get rid of the chill from the winter air. It's gotten into my bones. Whenever I think I'm finally getting warm, the... the draugur appears in my mind and it's like my marrow turns into slivers of ice."

Finnr's head shot up at my words. He nearly got to his feet.

"Did it curse you while you were at home?"

"I don't think it did."

41

"Good," said Finnr, baring his teeth and then lying back down. "If it's not a curse… I know something that might help make the cold go away. What do you feel when you think of the ice slivers?"

"Cold," I said, smirking.

Finnr gave an odd wheezing sound that I supposed was his laugh.

"Besides that. What do you feel in your chest?"

Breathing deep, I focused on how my body felt as I held the picture of the draugur in my mind.

"Embarrassment."

"Let that go. Just breathe it out and let it escape through your skin. Like this." He took a huge breath, his body expanding, and then let it out in one, smooth stream. I raised my eyebrows. "Trust me." Together, we inhaled, then exhaled, and I imagined the embarrassment leaving my body. The tension in my chest released, as if something heavy that had been sitting on it was now gone. It was amazing. Then my shoulders and ribs tightened, as if clenching together, and powerful emotion filled them so quickly that it startled me. I looked at Finnr.

"That just made it worse."

"Why, what do you feel now?"

"Anger. Rage." As much as I tried to keep my voice under control, the feeling came through and shook it. I scrabbled at it, trying to pull it back, but it sat in my body like a burning coal.

"Let that go, too, the same way as before." He started to inhale, then cut it short when he saw that I wasn't joining him. Everything inside me was screaming. "What's wrong?"

"I don't want to let it go."

"Really?" The fire spit, punctuating his question.

"No. I don't know." I frowned, trying to find a way to describe the confusion within me. "It's too strong to just breathe out like that. It's… it's like it's part of me."

"Nothing like that is a part of you," said Finnr, his voice as hard as mountain stone. "It will leave if you tell it to." He spoke with such certainty that I decided to at least try, to at least imagine the anger leaving while I breathed.

It did. It and everything that had held it, so completely that I couldn't help wondering if magic were involved.

"How do you come to learn about such things? This is almost like the work of God, or something supernatural, at least."

Finnr only shifted into a more comfortable position.

"What do you feel now?" he asked. I turned inward and, as I listened to my heart, tears started to flow from my eyes, and my chest ached. Was it sadness? No, something deeper than that. Hollower.

"I feel grief." It was as if I had a mouth inside of me, one that pulled with a powerful force, trying to consume me with jagged teeth.

Finnr's voice was gentle: "Let it go." We breathed in tandem, my hand on his side to keep me steady as the emotion passed through me and away. The merry crackling in the fireplace came soft to the forefront of my attention, as did the slow motion of Finnr's flank as he breathed. I was at peace. It felt like my heart was a field that had just been removed of stones.

"There's nothing left. But I'm still cold."

"Yes. But, understand, all the things keeping you cold have left you now. All that's left is to etch in something new, something that will keep you in another way of being." The blanket hung loose around me. I was hardly aware of its presence. All my intent had narrowed onto this new lightness that had entered my body. My heart felt like it could leap like a flame itself, except that it would never have to come back down.

"How do I do that?"

"You are Dagný, full of warmth and light. Say that about yourself like it's true."

"That's all?"

"That's all."

I did, savouring the words, their flavour on my tongue and lips. They settled on me, penetrated through to the deepest parts of my being, dispelling anything that might protest. It felt so real that I shrugged off the blanket and stood. At first, the ice in my bones flared outwards like chains trying to pull me back down. I ignored it and listened only to the new words that had sunk into my heart, repeating them like a prayer.

"I am Dagný, full of warmth and light."

Bit by bit, the cold melted and was gone.

"That was incredible," I said as I wrapped my arms around myself.

"How do you feel?" Finnr asked as though he were celebrating the arrival of a blessing.

"Free. I feel free."

CHAPTER SIX:

Homespun and Home Made

That night, for the first time since I'd left my family, I slept in a bed. The mattress rose up to embrace me as I lay down. Though I hadn't been uncomfortable in front of the fire, sleeping in a real bed was heaven, so much so that I wasn't sure I would be able to leave it when the morning came. But that held nothing compared to the bright music that had filled my heart since my conversation with Finnr. He had given me a miracle. A small one, I knew, and yet its size did nothing to diminish its power. Where had he learned such a thing? How had he known it would work to such perfection?

It occurred to me that I was staying not with a polar bear, but with an angel. Only such a being could know secrets like this. Or God could.

I didn't care what Finnr was. For the first time since the draugur had started its haunting, I was warm. That was all that mattered. I burrowed into the blanket like a small animal beneath the snow and smiled.

As sleep was about to take me, I remembered that I had left the lamps burning. The realization shot me straight to consciousness and, groaning, I sat up and pushed aside the blanket. At that moment, all the lights in the room extinguished, as if an invisible breath had crossed them all at once. I slid back down. Breathed in. Breathed out. Nothing more happened. It must have been part of the magic here, or else Finnr had his own silver bell, which he had used to put out all the light in the castle. I pulled the blanket back over me, lay on my side, and let every muscle relax. My thoughts ran around with no particular purpose, but they soon let go and let silent.

Sleep had started to fill my mind with wool again when the bed moved beneath me. My eyes shot open as the mattress shifted, the blanket was lifted, and someone lay down next to me. I lay rigid, breath caught in my throat, waiting to find out what this person would do next. They got comfortable, all without touching me, then became still. Heart crashing against my ribs, I held the blanket close to my chest. Nothing happened. They had fallen asleep.

God! I felt like I was about to cry. *GOD!*

There's nothing to worry about.

There is someone *in bed with me.*

Silence. Or maybe the faint sound of laughter. I couldn't tell which, so I decided it was the former.

God, what do I do?

You're in bed at night. As far as I understand, people in this situation generally sleep. I had to have heard that wrong. There was a person sleeping next to me, sharing the same bed, sleeping under the same blanket. God wouldn't act so cavalier about something like this. That had to have been my imagination.

46

Either that, or he was telling me that this would have happened every night here, had I been sleeping in this bed rather than in front of the fire. Was the response to do with the peace that surpasses all understanding that Father Símon preached about? If it was, he was right. This surpassed anything that might even pass as understanding.

God?

But he had faded into the background and I could no longer hear him. The person next to me continued to sleep. I turned carefully, wanting to see who it was, but the darkness was so complete that I couldn't even see the bed beneath me. It appeared I had no other choice but to follow God's advice.

It was a long night.

As winter faded into spring, I became used to my nighttime visitor, even waiting until they climbed into bed before I joined them in sleep. Of course, I wanted to know who or what they were, but the lamps always went out before they came, and I had nothing to light them with. One night, I even brought a lamp to the room with the large fireplace, but the fire was out as well, and I could find nothing to start it, not even kindling. It worried me a great deal at first, and I slept very little for the first few weeks, convinced that this person would harm me during the night. They didn't. All they seemed to want was to sleep, and they had already left by the time I awoke. The first night, I wondered if I had dreamed my visitor, but the other side of the bed was still wrinkled and a little warm.

For some reason, I could never bring myself to mention any of this to Finnr. It was as if my throat would close up even just thinking about telling him. He never spoke of it, either.

Strange as this was, it didn't affect our friendship, which had started to grow ever since that conversation by the fire. We spent most of the day together, exploring the castle without the help of the bell, playing tafl, or swimming in the ocean. With my father being a poor fisherman, I had little experience with swimming, so Finnr taught me how to float and hold my breath. He taught me that I could use my arms as well as my legs, and how to swim while keeping my head above water. Sometimes, what he showed me wouldn't translate well from polar bear to human, and I would end up doing something ridiculous, but he would only laugh and we would find a way to adjust the motion. When we had had enough, we would sit on the beach. I would be freezing, even wrapped in a blanket, and he would be perfectly content, joking about it until I left in mock anger to dry off and change.

I found myself far more relaxed and spontaneous in those months than I had ever been in my entire life. It would be easy to blame it on the lack of work, and I thought often that must be it, but there was more to it than that. Living in the castle, with the magic of the bell to provide my every need, and Finnr keeping me company, was like being a child. I didn't worry about the future. I didn't think much about the past. We lived in the present, savouring time like honey. It was something about the air of the place that filled me with contentment.

I suppose it was all too idyllic, too unfathomable to last. As the mountains turned from white to green and the wildflowers dotted the grass and rock with colour, thoughts of my family would jar me out of my enjoyment. I wondered how they were, if Finnr had really brought them his promised wealth. He would leave the castle often, and I assumed he did so to get his own food, for I never saw him eat, or perhaps it was to help my family in whatever way a polar bear could. Still, the worries in my mind grew in number like the flowers on the mountains.

"What's wrong, Dagný?" Finnr watched my hands as I picked imaginary lint from my sleeves. We had been lying on the rug in the library, telling each other our favourite tales. I'm not sure why he had a library (neither of us could read) except perhaps because of the smell of the books and how they looked in the light that poured in through the windows that overlooked the ocean.

He had just finished telling me a story about Oðin, in which he had hung himself from the World Tree for nine days in order to gain wisdom. I had told that story to Kaj often, and we would talk about how Oðin's sacrifice compared with the crucifixion of Jesús. He had loved to hear about the old, pagan gods, and how they had shadowed the truths of the Bible.

"Nothing." I bit my lip.

"That's not true."

"I know it's not," I snapped. "I just couldn't think of anything else to say."

"Ah." He sat up, and I went from removing lint to smoothing wrinkles. Before long, I sat up, too, and listened to the distant sound of the pounding waves as they tried, over and over, to bring the cliff crashing down. Finnr shook himself, scratched his side, then lay back down again.

"I want to go home," I said, my words so small in that space reserved for the preservation of speech.

"You want to what?" asked Finnr as his ears pricked up.

"I need to visit my family, Finnr. I haven't seen them for so long. I worry about them." I sat up and leaned against him.

"There's no need to worry," he soothed. His words rumbled through his body. "They are well, just like I promised they would be. I drove the draugur back to death and your family's wealth has returned." All the books seemed to be watching us, their mysterious knowledge held like magic between their covers.

Father Símon had tried to teach me how to read, but I had never been able to make the letters stay still. I had a good memory, though, and would learn as much as I could by listening, committing entire Norse sagas and books of the Bible to heart. My family had enjoyed listening to me tell those stories in the evening before we went to bed, and my sisters had stopped teasing me about my inability to read once I'd recited to them all the writings of Jesaja.

"That doesn't matter. I miss them. I can't stop thinking about what they're doing, or if they miss me. I crave my home," I said.

Finnr huffed and scratched his nose.

"I don't like it… but, if you really want to go that badly, I will take you to them. We'll go tomorrow, if you want."

"Thank you," I said, expecting to feel relieved at his agreement. Instead, tension curled around my heart, a serpent poised to strike. As far as I was concerned, he had changed his mind too easily.

CHAPTER SEVEN:
My Mother Worries

Finnr stopped at the edge of the fields and lay down so that I could dismount. The rye had already started to sprout, its tender shoots beautiful as they rose from the earth. In the pastures, sheep and cows grazed on new grass. Their smell wafted to me, brought by a faint breeze. My heart swelled, but my mind warned me that this was merely evidence that someone lived on the farm, and not necessarily my family. I searched the fields and the buildings for people. There, by the barn, stood my father, wearing the bright red hat that Mother's mother had made for him after he had nearly gotten lost in the snow one winter.

"When you lose your way, we'll find you," she'd said to him. Her opinion of his abilities had never been high, and this had only confirmed it, or so Mother told me whenever she recounted the story. I smiled.

"Dagný, before you go…" Finnr handed me my bag of presents, objects from the castle that I'd found over the months that were all somehow perfect for each of my family members. The silver bell hadn't brought me them. It was as if they'd been hidden away so that I would be able to experience the thrill of finding them. For Father, there was a new red hat.

"Thank you." I slung it on my shoulder and started on my way.

"Also." He pawed the ground. "Your mother will want to speak to you alone. Promise me you won't do that, and that you won't speak of anything…" Anything that happened after the sun had gone down. Even though he had never mentioned my visitor, it was the only thing that my mother didn't already know about, and the one she would object to the most. I wished I could find out what Finnr knew about the person who shared my bed each night. I wished he would just say if it was him. I wouldn't have minded. All this mystery, though, this secrecy —it made me doubt.

"I won't let her, don't worry."

"Thank you." He ducked his head. Then, without another word, he left. I sighed, whether out of happiness or something else, I didn't know, and headed towards my father. He must have seen me because his back abruptly straightened and he dropped whatever he had been carrying. I smiled and waved.

"Pabbi!"

"Dagný!" His shout came loud, so much so that he might have been standing right next to me. My smile widened and I started to jog to the barn. Father yelled towards the house. "Dagný's here! Quick, she's here!"

Mother's exasperated "What?" flew back at him, her usual response when someone interrupted her while she worked. Then: *"Dagný!"* She ran out of the house, followed by my sisters, save for Eir. Seeing me, my mother shrieked, then raced towards me to envelop me in her arms. I dropped my bag to return the embrace.

Human touch.

That evening, Mother made us a feast. Fermented eggs, skyr, dried fish with butter, early carrots… I ate until I felt full, and then ate a little more. The silver bell could bring me food that tasted adequate, but it couldn't bring my mother's cooking.

Although everyone still had work to do, we spent as much time as we could to relax, play, and simply be in each other's presence. I helped with the work, despite Mother's protests that visitors weren't supposed to do chores, and talked with Father while we tended the fields and the animals. I even brought cheese to Eir, who had gotten married only a few weeks before to a very sweet young man.

Nearly everyone who had lived in the village before had returned with the warmth. Auðun had come to see how my family fared once the snow started to melt, only to discover that they had thrived, living off of gifts of food that had appeared on the doorstep at intervals during the winter, and were starting to plant the rye and vegetables. He had then sent back word to everyone else, who then returned to their homes. Father Símon, the first to leave, had also been the first to come back, bringing with him animals as both a gift and an apology to my father. The day before I left, I went to visit Auðun, to thank him for coming back. I was still angry at him for everything he had done, and how he had left with the other villagers, but he had still cared enough to find out if we were well. When I was about to leave, he stopped me and said:

"I didn't want to leave you and your family when… when you had your trouble. It took your father nearly a day to convince me that you would be fine. I didn't want to abandon you. This past winter was one of the hardest in my life because of feeling that you and your sisters thought that I had left for the same reasons as all the others. Could you—" he paused to wipe tears from his eyes. "Could you find it within yourself to forgive me?"

Oh, Uncle Auðun. "Yes. With all my heart, yes." I still didn't want to forgive him, but he had held onto his sins enough for the both of us. We embraced and, as I exhaled, I imagined my anger and hurt leaving, like I had with the chill that night in the castle. It did, and a lump of iron disappeared from my stomach, leaving my entire body to feel nothing but light. I hummed to myself the entire walk from his house.

When I returned home, though...

Mother stood alone by the door to the house and beckoned to me. Remembering Finnr's warning, I searched for the rest of my family, only to find that my father and sisters were out in the fields.

"Come, let's speak alone. We haven't seen each other in so long," my mother said, gesturing towards the house. Finnr had been right. Of course he had; I could have predicted this, knowing my mother. How he knew, though, I could not figure out.

"There's nothing to say we can't talk about any other time," I said quietly and turned to leave. Mother grabbed my arm.

"Please, Dagný, I miss you, and I'm worried about you. You say you're well, but you look like you're keeping a secret and I want to be sure you're safe." She pulled me inside, her grip firm, and I had no choice but to follow. Closing the door behind us, my mother sat on one of the beds. I did the same. "What's really going on with that bear?"

"I've told you everything." I kept my attention on my hands.

"This is ridiculous! I knew this whole situation would be bad for someone. Yes, the bear kept his promise and we have wealth again, but you don't seem well, Dagný! I know you say nothing about yourself unless directly asked, but you've avoided answering any of our questions properly as if you might catch disease from speaking." Passion came from her in waves. It was hard not to glance up and see what was written on her face, but I couldn't do it. She would break me open and all would be revealed. I had never been able to keep secrets from my mother when she had set out to discover what they were.

When I was five, I'd stolen a candy from one of the children at church. She always got treats from her parents to enjoy while we all sat through Father Símon's sermons, so I thought she wouldn't notice that one had gone missing. Mother saw afterwards how uncomfortable I looked and asked me what was wrong. I tried to tell her nothing had happened, but she pulled the truth out of me like a tooth and soon had me apologize to the girl and her brother, in front of the rest of their family. Just thinking about her expression as I had confessed about the stolen candy still made my cheeks pink with shame.

Keeping my voice as even as possible, I told her everything about my nighttime visitor. How they would come into my bed after the lights had gone out of their own accord. How they would be gone by morning, with only mussed bed sheets to show their presence. How I had never seen their face, didn't know what

55

they were or who they were, and how I had simply had to let it happen. She sat for a very long time, rocking back and forth, her brow wrinkled. I waited, helpless.

"Oh, Lord have mercy! I knew the power behind that beast was unholy."

"They don't do anything! They only sleep!" I leaned forward, knuckles white from their grip on the bed. If it was Finnr... even if it wasn't Finnr, I didn't want any harm to come to him because of this person. It may have already come but, if I could minimize the damage in any way, I would.

"You can't go back."

"And bring back the draugur? Mamma!"

"You're right." She sat back with a thud. "You're right. But you have to find out what is sleeping next to you at nights. What if it's a troll?"

"This isn't some Christmas story," I said, but I shivered as my imagination lit up with images. For the last few months, I'd been living with a talking polar bear. My doubts about trolls didn't hold as strong as they used to.

"No, but it's still something to worry about. We can't accept the help of a creature that allows you to sleep next to a monster every night. You must find out what is sleeping with you. For me?" My mother tried to smile, but the corners of her mouth refused to lift.

"Fine," I whispered. "I'll do it."

That night, she gave me a small candle which I could hide under my nightclothes, and flint to light it. I dutifully stowed them away with my belongings, cheeks burning all the while. The

56

next day, when Finnr came to bring me back to the castle, he asked me if I'd spoken with my mother alone. I told him that I had, expecting him to react in anger. He didn't. He just sighed.

CHAPTER EIGHT:
A Drop of Candle Wax

I kept the candle and flint under my nightgown as I crept into bed, slipping under the blanket like a knife between ribs. It had crossed my mind that the person who shared my bed every night was really Finnr, magicked to keep his weight from breaking the bed, and no human at all. I would see nothing but the embarrassed face of a polar bear, whatever that might look like. If that was so, then it was best not to even try this… and yet I couldn't erase from my mind my mother's fears, which had settled in and sprouted, producing even more horrors than she had hinted at.

The lights went out. I kept as still as I could while the person climbed onto the bed and settled under the blanket with me. I waited, heart pounding, as they moved restlessly. After an immeasurable number of heartbeats, they finally stilled. Even so, I had to wait. Their breathing slowed and became shallow. They had fallen asleep.

Hands clumsy with haste, I pulled the candle out from my nightgown and tried to light it. The first time, I didn't get a spark. The second time, it caught on my clothing and I had to press my fingers against it, whispering curses as it burnt the skin. The third time, the spark found the wick. I put down the flint and shielded the open flame with my hand.

It was a man.

He lay face towards me, his expression sweet with dreams. His sandy hair stuck out in sleep-mussed confusion on the pillow. I leaned over to better see what he looked like and, before I could stop them, three drops of tallow fell from the candle and onto his shirt. I snatched back the candle, hoping the incident hadn't been enough to wake him. I was wrong.

The man gaped at the cooling tallow, his face a mask of horror.

"What have you done?" he asked, his voice deep and rough. "You have brought destruction on me. If you had but stayed with me a year, I would have been free from the curse. With you here, it was already weakening —I could return to nearly my true self at night. But now the one who cursed me will return to take me, to make me one with her daughter."

Finnr? A wisp of cold snaked around my heart. He shook his head, lost in his words.

"You may think marriage nothing so great as to call it destruction, but you do not know where I will be imprisoned. I have been enslaved by your action." Tears began to flow from his eyes, making rivers through the soft crevices of his face. I couldn't help but cry as well. A storm had lodged itself inside my chest. What had I done?

"You have been so good to me and my family, and this is how I repay you? I am so sorry, Finnr. Please, tell me how I can help you. Tell me how I can save you." Tallow dripped onto my hand, hot enough to burn, but I held onto the candle. There was nowhere to put it.

He shook his head and took the candle gently from me. "You can't."

"I won't accept that. There has to be some way. There has to be. You were my angel from God; you can't fall to a curse. Even if you were imprisoned, I will come and I will free you." I wrapped my arms around Finnr. He felt so small, so childlike; I could hardly stand how frail he seemed. "Tell me how I can save you, Finnr. Tell me where to go."

"Even if you knew where I was held, you wouldn't be able to come and find me. It is in the land east of the sun and west of the moon. It would take you more than a lifetime to reach it." He shuddered. "Let me go. She is here."

In that instant, there came a high, keening screech, and the air around us became as thick as stone. A pale woman appeared, in the midst of a great rushing as if surrounded by a storm, but there was no wind. Her swollen face split into a grin at the sight of my candle and she reached out for Finnr with glistening hands. He sat up, and I could feel with agonizing clarity every creak of the bed as he reached out to touch her.

I wanted to scream at him, to pull his arm away, but whatever enchantment held the air, held me as well. I could only stare and fear. Finnr smiled at me sadly, tiredly. Their hands touched, and a force hit me, shocking my senses empty and my breath silent. Everything evaporated, leaving only darkness.

Part Three
The four winds and what they said

CHAPTER NINE:
Finding East Wind

I stood alone in a forest of black trees under a black sky. Wind blew in their heights and, for one sickening moment, I thought that I hadn't really left the castle. Only the lack of pounding against a cliff told me that what I saw was true. The castle had vanished and Finnr with it, taken by the pale woman.

She had looked like a draugur. Some of the stories said they were pale, as if the blood had been emptied from their bodies and had taken all their colour with it. Was that why Finnr had been able to stop the one that had haunted my family, because this other draugur had given him that power along with the curse? No, that made no sense. When people had accused Jesús of using Satan's power to cast out demons, he had said: "A house divided against itself cannot stand".

And here I was, alone in the woods because I had given in to the division in myself. I would not let it end like this. Even if I were the only one to try and change anything, I refused to let this be the end.

For the rest of the night and most of the next day, I walked. East of the sun, west of the moon: It didn't make any sense to me but, surely, if I found a town, I would also find someone who could lead me in the direction I needed to go. As the sun began to set and the sky poured drizzle through the trees, I found a road and, after leaving the forest, a small turf house. I shivered, not only from the rain, and trudged up to the door. When I knocked, an old woman opened it.

"Oh, poor child. Come in, get warm." She took in my wet clothes, the circles that had most certainly appeared under my eyes. "Stay the night."

"I can't. I need to travel as far as I can today. But, could you tell me, do you know the way to the land that's east of the sun and west of the moon?"

The woman frowned, looking at me like my grandmother would when I was coming down with a fever.

"I've never heard of such a land," she said gently. My shoulders drooped.

"Sorry for wasting your time." I started to leave.

"Wait!"

I stopped. The woman chewed her lip and frowned. "You wouldn't happen to be looking for someone would you? Someone… this may sound strange… someone you're trying to rescue?"

Mouth open and eyes wide, I could do nothing more than stare at her for a long time. She shook her head. "I must be wrong, never mind."

"No, you're correct," I said, and it was her turn to stare. "Why do you ask?"

"I have something for you. Ten years ago, I had a dream about a young woman who would come to my door. She was searching for someone she needed to rescue. In my dream, when I greeted her, a voice told me to give her this—" She bent down to pick up from behind the door a small apple that appeared to be made of gold. I couldn't think of anything to say. The woman smiled awkwardly. "There's also something I'm supposed to tell you:

"The islands have seen it and fear;

The ends of the earth tremble.

They approach and come forward;

They help each other

And say to their companions, 'Be strong!'"

I knew that passage; it was from the Bible, the book of Jesaja. The next parts of it flowed through my mind automatically, slowing at these words:

"But you, Israel, my servant…

I took you from the ends of the earth,

From its farthest corners I called you.

I said, 'You are my servant';

I have chosen you and have not rejected you.

So do not fear, for I am with you."

Tears welled up from deep within my chest, as if some hard place in my heart had broken open and a flood poured out through it, leaving healing in its wake. I wanted to recite this to the woman, explain why what she had said had touched me. The words to describe it didn't come, so I just stood there, tears streaming down my face, unable to speak, caught in the power of the moment.

"I'm sorry if that was strange—"

"No." I hugged her fiercely. "It was beautiful. Thank you."

65

"There's one more thing," she said, still hesitant despite the wetness that had also come to her eyes.

"What?"

"I don't know where this land is that you're looking for, but if you follow the road to its far end," she pointed, "it will take you a friend of mine. Tell her that Björg sent you. I think that she will be able to help you and, even if she can't, God is with you. He will lead you." At the phrase 'God is with you', I wanted to cry again, for joy. How did she know? How did she know any of this?

God, is this you? He didn't speak, but I was sure he was smiling.

Ten years. She had waited ten years.

By the time I reached Björg's friend's house, night had covered the eye of the sun with sleep, and my stomach had begun to pang with emptiness. I knocked on the door, and it was answered by a middle-aged woman in a nightdress.

"Björg sent you, am I correct?" she said, eyeing me with concern.

"Yes," I said. Björg must have mentioned her dream to her friend. "She said—"

"That I might be able to help you find someone, yes," she said. I opened my mouth, but she shook her head. "Come in, but don't say anything about your business yet. You will stay here tonight. My husband and children are out of town right now, so I have plenty of room and food for you. In the morning, we will talk. No more of this walking all hours by yourself in the rain."

I tried to protest again, which only led to more negations. She was like a benevolent force of nature. I had no choice but to let her have her way if I wanted her help.

After a full night of sleep and an admittedly much-needed meal, I explained to her my problem.

"East of the sun and west of the moon, you say?" she asked, her index finger pressed against her lips and eyebrows lowered.

I nodded. She shrugged and lifted both hands, palms facing me.

"I can't help you find it, but I do have something for you: You're going there to right a wrong, one that you committed in a moment of fear." She paused to drink her milk, without even looking at me for confirmation. "You think that going and doing this will repay what you've done. It won't. But that's not the point. Go there anyways, succeed, and emerge in victory over the power of death. But let go of the shame before you do, or it will kill you." With that, she nodded to herself and finished her milk.

"How can you know this?" I asked.

"I'm just a God-fearing woman, like yourself. Nothing more than that. Now, if you go up over the hill…" She then proceeded to rattle off a series of directions from her house to the house of someone else —I missed the name— who apparently had information that would help me to find the land east of the sun and west of the moon. Once she'd finished listing them all and I was still trying to impress them on my mind, she gave me a pack, into which she had put food, clothing, and a tiny golden carding comb which she said might be useful. Then she sent me on my way.

"I'm sorry for the haste, but, if you don't hurry, you won't get there in time. He's a bit of a flighty fellow." She chuckled.

For the most part, I kept the directions clear in my mind, coming to all the landmarks she had mentioned, but her words deteriorated quickly. A little after noon, I came to a fork in the road. One direction led to a dead tree and, after that, my destination. For a moment, I stared at the road and tried to reconstruct what she had said. The only thoughts that came to mind were how she had told me to hurry. I threw my hands into the air, then headed left.

"You're going the wrong way," said a girl with unusually fair hair. She sat on the fence that lined the left side of the road, legs swinging. I didn't remember seeing her there before.

"I'm looking for a dead tree that hangs over the road. Past it should be the house of the person I'm trying to get to."

"And you're going the wrong way. It's the road to the right that you need to take." As she finished speaking, a wind blew, picking up my hair so that it flew towards the right fork. It could have been coincidence. Just like Björg's dream and her friend's knowledge could have been coincidence.

"Thank you." It seemed inadequate, but what else could I say? It made me think of how Father had responded to Finnr's 'Good evening' with 'The same to you' all that time ago.

"Before you go…" the young woman slipped down off the fence and handed me a miniature loom made entirely from gold.

"I don't understand," I said.

"You will." She smiled and then vanished. I looked around, painfully aware of my heartbeat, only to find that I had somehow been transported to a path that led to a house atop a hill.

The door opened.

CHAPTER TEN:
Neither West nor South

I put the gold loom into my pack, not sure if I was about to meet a friend or foe, and wanting my hands to be free if it were the latter. Out of the house came a tall man whose body appeared to be made of wind. No, not appeared. It *was* made of wind, wind somehow made visible. It was like the trembling of water, like seeing the sound of leaves in a storm. As he moved, it flowed like muscles in his limbs and torso, and, when he stood still, it shivered through him in anticipation of action. The man saw me, raised his eyebrows, and stopped in the doorway.

"I am East Wind," he said. "What's your name?"

"I'm... you're the east wind?" Any minute now, a Christmas troll would come out and introduce itself as well. I resisted the urge to look over my shoulder.

"Yes, I am. Does that bother you? I could leave —I was about to go anyway."

"No, no, it doesn't bother me. My name's Dagný, and I think I was sent here..." I didn't know what to say. It was hard to know what to do in such a situation.

"Do you want some tea? I can put some honey in it, if you want."

"Tea?"

"It's a warm drink, very calming. I picked it up in my travels and I liked it so much that I always keep a store… I forget that not everyone knows about it."

"I think I'll not have the tea, thank you. I- I need your help." Although I still wasn't sure if it was East Wind I was meant to see, I couldn't think of a better person to ask about this land. If anyone would know, it would be the wind. The wind! Perhaps the winds had known I would be coming. I remembered how my hair had been blown in the right direction. And how the breeze had picked up when Finnr had stopped to gaze at the northern lights. And how, when I'd gone out to the hills after the funeral, the wind had led me out to the river and beyond. Had the winds always been with me this whole time? "I'm looking for the land that's east of the sun and west of the moon. Someone I know is there, and I need to find him."

"There's a land that's east of the sun *and* west of the moon?" East Wind leaned against the door, exhaling noisily. "I wish I could help you, but I've never even heard of such a land, much less seen it. Are you sure that's where it is?"

"That's where he told me he'd be."

"Odd. Then again, it's odd that you'd show up on my doorstep like this. How did you even get here?" He furrowed his eyebrows, managing to look more comical than serious.

"I—"

"Bah, that doesn't matter," he said, waving his hand. "You need help, and so I will help you. I may not know where this land is, but I'm sure my brother will. May I take you to him?"

I nodded. What else could I do?

East Wind stepped away from the house and turned. As I watched, a pair of wings appeared along his back and began to unfold. They stretched out, each longer than he was tall and, once they had reached their full spread, he beckoned to me.

"Climb on my back, and I'll fly you."

"On your back?"

"Can you think of another way for me to take you there? Come on."

Once I had climbed up, East Wind leapt into the air, his wings pumping, bringing us up and up until he could simply soar. The land looked like a tapestry, with trees the size of toys growing from the spaces in its weave. I would normally be afraid of falling, but this… we were so far up that it didn't even feel real. I wasn't afraid.

Too soon for my taste, East Wind descended, landing by a large turf house, beside which stood another man made of wind. I slid off the back of East Wind and stood beside him as he folded his wings.

"Hello, brother!" East Wind waved to the other man.

"Hello!" East Wind's brother gave him a hug, then stepped back to look at me. "I am West Wind. Who are you?"

"I'm Dagný. I'm here to ask for your help." My stomach growled.

"And my food, it seems," he said lightly. I blushed.

"No, I have my own," I said, then I told him why I had come to his house. He frowned and scratched his head.

"I've never heard of a land like that."

"Wouldn't South Wind know, then?" asked East Wind. "We're too used to our directions to notice if something strange lay upon them, like tea." He winked at me.

"You're right. South Wind might know." West Wind turned to me. "I can take you to him, if you want. He's often home, and I know the way better than East Wind does."

"Do not!" East Wind glared at his brother. West Wind only rolled his eyes.

"Will you come with me?" he asked.

"Yes, I'll come." What else was there to say?

"Good. Brother, make yourself at home if you wish but, whatever you do, don't touch the chai. It's mine."

East Wind stuck out his tongue, then headed into the house.

As West Wind flew, I could see the land beneath us, now that the sky had cleared of clouds. The mountains rose as if from water, their slopes formed from rushing upwards through the waning power of the Flood to stand on their own feet. In another land, far from Iceland, another mountain had at the same time held on its top Nóa's ark, cradling it as the waters receded and the land became dry again. I had never been able to imagine such a thing until seeing those mountains from above. I only caught a glimpse of them before we started rushing down into one of the green valleys that nestled between the towers of rock and snow. West Wind's wings were nearly folded flat to his back. We fell so fast that it felt as if my face were deforming. The mountains hurtled toward us, and I closed my eyes, praying that he would open his wings before we hit the rocks and our insides rained onto the valleys between them.

With a lurch, West Wind stopped the descent. He coasted for a few moments, then landed gently. I opened my eyes and jumped to the ground. We stood on a small hill between the mountains, on top of which stood a cozy, if somewhat disheveled-looking house.

"I have to go on an errand, but South Wind lives in that house. Just tell him that I brought you here, but had to leave before I could introduce the two of you. He'll understand. I'm not around often." He waved, leapt into the air, and flew away. I took a breath and walked up to the door of the house of South Wind. My hands were shaking.

God? It occurred to me that what I wanted him to say didn't matter. No one I had spoken to had said anything I wanted them to say, and yet they had either spoken with his words, or acted with his power. Or, at least, power I had never seen before. I let go of deciding which words I would accept from him. *I want to hear what you want to say.*

I'm with you. And it was enough.

Thanks. God with me, I knocked on the door. South Wind opened it and stared down at me with gold eyes. He was taller even than West Wind, who stood nearly a head above East Wind.

"Hello," he said. "Why are you here?" The muscles in my shoulders and neck tensed. His tone hadn't been unfriendly, but it hadn't been friendly, either.

"West Wind brought me here, then had to leave to go on an errand."

"To get home before East Wind drinks all his tea, rather. I know he didn't say it to you, but we're brothers. I've known them

73

their entire lives; they always do this." South Wind laughed. "Come inside, and we'll talk by the fire."

"No, thank you. If you can help me, I don't want to be slowed and, if you can't… well, I don't want to be slowed."

"Fair enough. What can I help you with?" His tone softened.

Again, I explained I was looking for the land that was east of the sun and west of the moon, and that I had to find someone there.

"And so West Wind brought you to me?"

I nodded.

"Let me guess, you went to East Wind first, and he brought you to West Wind, who brought you to me?"

I nodded again. South Wind grimaced.

"My brothers are a pair of idiots. Affable idiots, but idiots nonetheless. They should have taken you straight to North Wind. He's the oldest and strongest of the four of us. Even if I and the other two have never heard of lands like the one you speak of (and I haven't heard of it, I'm sorry to say), if they exist, he's not only heard of them, but been to them. I will take you to him, without delay, and scold my brothers later. Excuse me." I moved aside and he came out of the house, head bent to avoid hitting the doorframe. He unfolded his wings quickly, more so than either of his brothers had, and lifted me onto his back.

If riding West Wind had been frightening, riding South Wind was terror. I clung to him, lost in the speed of his flight. The land rushed by and we came so near to hitting trees, mountains, or houses that I had to close my eyes. Before we had travelled long enough for me to panic, South Wind slowed. I opened my eyes as he lighted on the side of a mountain, only a few steps away from a house carved into the rock. Around the house was a sizeable patch of grass and wildflowers, at the far edge of which sat the oldest and strongest of the winds.

CHAPTER ELEVEN:
The Riddle

North Wind sat with his back to us as if in thought. His hair melded with the bright wind of his body, which rushed through and around him in a muted howling. If his brothers were unusually tall, he was a giant, nearly twice as tall as I, with powerful arms and shoulders.

"Brother!" said South Wind, his voice warm with pleasure. He let me slip from his back as his wings folded away. "I didn't expect you to be home, with spring on its way." North Wind sighed, a long, ponderous breath, and stood to face us.

"Who has come to see me?" he asked, his eyes staring through me with icicles in their depths. He crossed his arms and tilted his head to one side. Beneath his arms, his beard curled and uncurled, flowing in tandem with the power of his body.

"This young woman," said South Wind, placing a hand on my shoulder, "Is searching for a man become a bear, so that she might save him from the fate she doomed him to." I squirmed beneath his touch, uncomfortable with such familiarity, and with the tragedy in his words. North Wind raised an eyebrow.

"You are that one?"

"Yes." I only realized after I'd spoken the full meaning of his words. Of both of their words. I hadn't mentioned any details about Finnr to South Wind.

"Then why have you come to me? If he is doomed, then why not just return home and enjoy peace with your family and friends?" He leaned over until his eyes were level with my face. "Why would you continue when it would be so much easier to ask me to take you back?" His eyes, a brilliant blue, searched mine.

"Must you do this, brother?" asked South Wind, who took his hand from my shoulder and used it to pull North Wind back. "She has come too far for us to doubt her conviction, or her purpose."

"I think not," said North Wind, but he straightened. He asked me: "What is your name?"

"Dagný."

"Your *full* name." North Wind's voice boomed, shaking the air around me. I stood as tall as I could and stared straight into his eyes.

"My name is Dagný Aradóttir. Is there any other unimportant information you wish to know?" The last sentence flew out before I could help it, but I let it hang in the air. It suited my mood. To my surprise, North Wind's arms fell to his sides and he laughed.

"Certainly not. A name is never unimportant, but I see now why you only gave me your first. You come to me as yourself, and only yourself. Come, sit. We shall negotiate." He gestured towards the grass beside him and sat with his back to us. South Wind clapped me on the back, smiling.

"You will find help from him, I'm sure of it," he said. "I will leave you to it, as I must attend my work. May you find the one for whom you search!" Wings unfolded from his back, bringing a warm draft with them.

"Thank you," I said and closed my eyes to let the wind wrap around me. When I opened them, he had flown away.

North Wind cleared his throat and shifted in place, so I sat by him. He had brought out a long, fat-bellied pipe and was smoking it with clear enjoyment. After a few puffs, he gave a long exhale and set the pipe down onto the grass. The smoke rose, sinuous, into the air, until the heat died and it dissolved into sky.

"In some parts of the world, they smoke a pipe as a symbol of peace before talking business. I find the practise useful," he said, then lay back, hands beneath his head.

"Do you carry it with you?" I asked. He chuckled.

"No. Today, I had it because I knew I would be doing business."

"How?" Had he been flying and saw us coming? If so, wouldn't South Wind have noticed his attention and gone towards him instead of bringing me all the way to his house? He waggled a finger at me.

"That isn't business. You need my help: Explain why." His tone made it clear that he would accept nothing less than everything and, considering that he already seemed to know about my search, it would be pointless to hide anything.

So, I told him. I told him how Kaj had died and returned. I told him how Finnr had given me a choice and I'd gone with him to save my family. I told him how I'd repaid that kindness.

He waited as my emotions overwhelmed me and poured out through my eyes and mouth in wailing. It was so easy to think about how to explain my motivations. Thoughts exist in a half-world, only partly real. Words, though, are substance. They remind us that our memories really happened, that we really did the things we'd rather forget. They pull them from the shadowlands and into the light of day.

"I'm sorry about the loss of your brother," said North Wind. "Death is a terrible thing." He paused, as if to let his words sink into my heart, which they did. What he said did nothing but confirm my own thoughts, but it was a comfort to hear the words from another.

"Thank you." I could barely hear myself. North Wind nodded, grave, then spoke again:

"About this land your Finnr has been taken to… 'east of the sun and west of the moon'. That's an odd phrase. No wonder my brothers could offer you no help. They do not travel behind the light."

"You don't know where it is," I said.

"Just because you don't know where something is doesn't mean you can't find out how to get there. Think of it like a riddle, if you like that sort of thing." He smiled. "We even have three clues."

"Three?" I could only count two.

"It's east of the sun," he put up one finger, "west of the moon," a second, "and it's *a* land, which means that its location is only one place." That was hardly a clue. He looked so pleased that I decided not to contest it, only his earlier point.

"Which means that that location is what those two directions have in common," I said.

He grinned, took a deep breath, and tapped against his chin with a forefinger.

"But how can they have a location in common when they each point outwards?" I asked. "That's like saying that a town is on both the east and west coast of Iceland. Tell me, how would one find how to get to a place with impossible directions?"

"It could be that he told you something impossible just to keep you away from him," North Wind said as he looked at the sky, eyes a little glazed. "But you don't believe that. If you had, you wouldn't be here. You wouldn't have come so far to find it unless you had hope that you could find this impossible place. But what is something that is both east of the sun and west of the moon?"

"If you don't know where it is, just tell me who to go to that will be able to tell me," I snapped. I didn't want to play a game. I just wanted an answer so that I could go where I needed to be and do what I needed to do. "That's what everyone else has done."

"I've blown across the face of the world, seen everything in it. Short of God, I'm the only one who can find this place for you," he responded cooly.

"Your brothers have, too, and none of them could tell me anything of use," I said, crossing my arms. I considered hitting him with his idiotic pipe, but I would have to reach over him to get it, and my arms were too short.

"Didn't they tell you I was the oldest and strongest of them all? More experience means more knowledge. Of course they wouldn't be able to help you and I would."

"Arrogant bastard!" I stood and stepped away.

"It's not arrogance if it's the truth," he called after me in a singsong voice. God, I wanted to wring his neck.

Sorry, God. I couldn't tell if his response was laughter or silence. I didn't care.

"Oh!" North Wind sat up as if he were a rake and someone had just stood on his tines.

"What?" I yelled.

"I figured it out! East of the sun, west of the moon… behind the light… if you went west of the sun and east of the moon, what would you find?"

"This world. Where we live."

"Exactly! 'Where we live.' Where the living are. Which means the land east of the sun and west of the moon is where the living *aren't.*"

"It's… what?" I said, frowning. He beckoned me to come sit next to him. I did.

"Niflheim, Yomi, Sheol, Hades… it's called by many names and described as many things." With a finger, he drew something in the dirt, my view of it blocked by his hand. "But it is only one place."

My breath came shallow. Part of me understood with terrible clarity what he was saying, but another covered its ears in fear. I tried to swallow with a dry throat, waiting for him to finish his sketch. His finger stopped moving and, after a pause to survey his work, he withdrew his hand.

An owl standing atop a skull.
My God.
The land of the dead.

CHAPTER TWELVE:
Foxfire

"I once blew an aspen leaf that far, but it took so much of my strength that I had to rest for days," North Wind said. "Even the faintest of breaths was beyond my ability. Do you really wish to go there? I can try and take you if you truly want it. The way will be hard and wild, and you will have to remain unafraid if you want to come through to the other side."

"Yes," I said without hesitation. "I want to go."

"You will ride through the light to the other side, no matter what lies there, no matter the madness of our travel? Your purpose is steadfast enough? *You* are steadfast enough?"

"With all my heart." If I could have shown it to him, it would have been shining like a star. I could feel my conviction, solidified after so many days of travel, after so much trouble, after so much hope. North Wind stroked his beard and stared at the setting sun, and then he nodded.

"If we are to do this, then we must give ourselves an entire day, and you look tired already from your journeying. You may spend the night in my house, and I will rest outside and keep watch for you."

"Thank you." North Wind opened the door and stepped

aside to let me inside.

"You may not think the same when you have arrived there."
I ignored his words and entered the house. Inside was a bed, a
fireplace, and not much else. The fireplace leapt and danced and
it hurt to look at it. It reminded me of the castle and that night
when Finnr and I had talked together for the first real time. My
breath shuddered in my lungs.

Ignoring the flames, I undressed and got into bed.
Exhaustion hit me as soon as I lay down, and my body tried to
melt into the mattress. My mind wouldn't let it. Everything that
had happened since that pale woman had taken Finnr rolled
around and around in my thoughts. It had waited politely in the
background since then, but now that I could truly rest, the
memories thronged around me, demanding attention.

Ten years. Björg had held onto that dream for ten years before
it came true. Where had that dream come from? Had God
planned all this? Or had he just known it would happen and then
prepared the way? Björg's friend had attributed her knowledge to
being God-fearing. Somehow, God had told her those things
either as she was saying them or as I was telling her my problem.

So, Björg had had a dream from God, and her friend could
hear him speak. Where did that leave the girl I'd met on the road?
Who was she? She hadn't even needed to ask me where I was
going; she had simply known. And then, afterwards...

I shook my head, trying to calm the thoughts so that I could
sleep. In the morning, I would be travelling to the land of the
dead. The last thing I needed was to be tired.

My stomach growled, louder than it had at West Wind's

house. Sighing, I got out of bed and took out the food Björg had given me. As I chewed a strip of dried fish, I tried to empty my mind of the storm of thoughts and questions. I tried to leave behind only the quiet contentedness that should lead to a restful sleep. Most of it faded into the background. Most of it. And even those thoughts didn't stay there peacefully.

God… What would I even ask him? Even if he spoke, I doubted he would fully answer my questions. Honestly, I didn't want him to answer. I had arrived at the house of North Wind. Tomorrow, I would be in the land of the dead. It didn't matter if he had helped me get here; I could accept this all as a result of my own effort.

Except that it did matter.

God?

Yes?

I don't know.

That's a good place to start. The fish nearly dropped out of my mouth. His voice had been so loud it was almost like I had heard him with my physical ears and not just with… whatever I usually heard him with. He didn't stop there, either: *Do you trust me?*

Of course. That was a lie, but one born out of habit. I had always been taught that I was supposed to trust God; that being a good person meant trusting him. It jarred me a little, that lie. I decided that my answer would become the truth for right then, just to see what might come out of it. Because he was with me.

I will tell you to do something soon. And everything I tell you to do, you are already able to do.

His words echoed through that night and my dreams until I

woke, and then they stepped aside in the faint roar of thunder to let me walk into the new day, and the journey on the back of North Wind.

North Wind and I spoke very little to each other. I didn't mind. My thoughts from the night before hadn't stopped churning, and he seemed to suffer a similar affliction. When he began to slow, I surfaced from the sleep of my thoughts, brushing away tangles of anxiety in favour of the cold familiarity of desperation.

We had come to an open barrow, around which shone an eerie white halo. North Wind hovered a moment before it, his wings pumping a wild heartbeat into the clouds.

"Are you afraid?" he asked.

"No, I'm not." Of course not. I couldn't be.

And so we entered the barrow, passing through to the other side of light.

Part Four
Behind the light

CHAPTER THIRTEEN:
Draugur Queen

The world roared as if in a windstorm. Darkness streamed by, somehow visibly moving. The sound penetrated to the marrow and shook my bones from within. Goosebumps arose on my skin as the deep cold made itself one with my body. People (or shadows of people) filled the howling emptiness around me, coming to and fro in meaningless movement. I closed my eyes against everything around me and pushed my face against North Wind, trying to distract myself with the simplicity of life, but he collapsed beneath me and I fell onto the stony ground.

With the storm of sensation around me, all I could do was curl up, eyes shut tight and hands pressed against my ears. I screamed at my surroundings in an effort to overwhelm it with the feel of my voice as it vibrated through my body. It helped a little. Eventually, I became used to the storm that was the land of the dead and, as a strong smell fades over time, the whirlwind that had no wind fell away from my perception.

When I could stand, I saw North Wind, lying faded and weak on the ground not far from me. His wings spread out behind him, mangled and wispy in the darkness. I knelt beside him and shook him by one shoulder until he opened his eyes. Instead of their normal blue, they had become nearly white with a dark ring that outlined where the colour had been. The sight of those washed-out eyes shocked me, and I flinched before I could gather myself and relax.

"Are you afraid?" North Wind asked, his breath faint. I shook my head. "Good. I thought you wouldn't be." His wings began to fold into his back, and he closed his eyes again. A pang stabbed through my heart.

"Wake up!" I shook him again, harder.

"I'm fine," he said. "I just need to rest a while before I can return. You're much heavier than an aspen leaf." He chuckled, then wheezed into a cough as the laughter became stronger than he could sustain. I gave a watery smile, even though he couldn't see it through closed eyes, and stood.

"I'll stand guard until you're ready." But he shook his head.

"There's no time. You've travelled long to find this place, and delaying any longer might mean disaster for both yourself and the one you've come to save. There is no one but the dead here, and I am the wind. They cannot harm me." He smiled and shooed me away.

"Thank you for your help. I don't know how I can ever repay you."

"Don't," he said. "Just save him."

I nodded, then surveyed the land to see if I could find anything that stood out. The shades around me obscured everything besides their movement and the storm of darkness. There did seem to be something rising above them, a silhouette of black against black, discernible only by its stillness. I took a deep breath, then headed towards it.

The darkness pushed and pulled me in every direction at once, as if it wanted me somewhere, but couldn't decide on a location. The shades bumped into me as they rushed by, sometimes passing through me, their constant movement that lead everywhere and nowhere, their faces devoid of expression. It felt like struggling through neck-high mud.

When I came to the still place in the black, I could see that it was a castle. Or shaped like one, at the very least, as it wasn't made of any material I knew. Its walls were the dark made smooth and solid. Dark made without opening, or none that I could see. The shades drifted by the walls, almost lingering the closer they came. One passed close to me.

"Excuse me," I said. It stopped and stared at me with vacant eyes. "Is there any way into this castle?"

"No admittance, by order of Queen Erlendsína."

"None?"

"Not until the wedding." The wedding! Finnr.

"When is the wedding?"

"Tomorrow." I looked up, but there was nothing above me to indicate that there was even a sky in this land. Any view was blocked by the raging dark.

"How will I know when it's…" the shade had gone. I could have questioned another, I suppose, but I had the feeling that the conversation would be equally unhelpful. Instead, I went up to the castle walls and started walking beside them, searching for a door, a window, anything that might show me a way in.

While the ground beyond the castle was flat and hard, the

ground near the walls was made of many small, brittle stones. They crunched beneath my feet as I rounded the first corner.

"Hejsan!" someone called from below. "Vem är det?" I stopped, my shoes scraping against the gravel. Near the foot of the castle was a semicircular barred window. A hand reached out of it and waved. I knelt down to see a man's face behind the bars. He smiled. "Förstår du mig?" I frowned. I didn't know any languages other than Icelandic, and I didn't want to agree (or disagree) to something I didn't understand. At the same time, I didn't want to leave, either. This man wasn't like the shades. He had actually spoken to me, called me over.

"Puhutko suomea?" said someone else. Looking further into the room behind the bars, I saw another man, along with between ten and twenty others. The first man glared at the second, who only shrugged.

"Norsk?" asked the first. That, I understood. I shook my head.

"Icelandic," I said. The man's eyes brightened.

"You speak Icelandic?" he said. I nodded. "And are you... are you alive?"

"Yes."

The man informed the others of this information in various languages. They all shouted, some weeping, all joyous. "Are you?"

"Yes! Yes, we are all alive here. We were taken captive by the queen, locked away months ago, for some. How is it that you are free? Can you help us escape?"

"I came here with the help of the north wind... I don't know if I could help you, especially since I don't even know how to get inside."

"The north wind? Is that a riddle, or are you avoiding answer?"

"North Wind brought me here. I rode on his back; it's as simple as that," I said. He opened his mouth, but I spoke before he could. "Disbelieve me if you want, but you're the one sitting in a castle in the land of the dead, having been brought here by a creature that was supposed to have only existed in pagan times." The man chuckled, then explained to the others what we were saying.

"Your Icelandic is very good," I said, filling the silence while I tried to think of how they might help me into the castle. If that were even possible. The man nodded.

"I'm Swedish, actually, but I spent many years in Iceland as a boy with my father —he was a trader. I took over his business when he died."

"Is that how you came here? How Erlendsína captured you?" One of the men in the back called out to the Swede. The others recreated a scene of languishing prisoners with practised swiftness.

"The princess, Ýrr, can be bribed with gold," said the Swede. "Just make it visible, and she will come. Now, go! Someone's coming."

CHAPTER FOURTEEN:

The Daughter's Weakness

I fled behind the castle. The shades pressed in around me, almost as if they were in distress. Their faces had inched toward unhappiness. Could they tell I was alive? They returned to their aimless rushing when I stopped and leaned against the back wall of the castle.

Not knowing what else to do, I took out the golden apple and started tossing it idly from hand to hand.

"Where did you get a trinket like that?" Above me, a young woman had poked her head out of one of the windows.

I tried to answer the way a shade would: "I've always had it." It had occurred to me that her knowing I was alive would not be to my advantage.

"Then you must be terribly bored with it," said the young woman without missing a beat. "What do you want for it?"

"It's not for sale, for gold or money." The mention of gold was nonsensical, true, but so was the idea of tomorrow in a land made of darkness. The young woman snorted.

"Well, if it's not for sale for gold or money, then what will you sell it for? Name your own price if you can, shade." My mind raced. The Swede had said that the princess could be bribed with gold, but how much would she be willing to do for such a small piece as this? No, I had to ask for something specific. Something simple.

"You may have it if I may visit for a time the man betrothed to you." The princess's peals of laughter echoed out into the black.

"Oh, you're a funny one. Yes, you can come in for a bit to see my Galdur. Just wait a bit, then come to the gate and I'll let you in." She withdrew into the castle again. Galdur? Not Finnr? He had said that he was called Finnr but nothing more. I took a deep breath and made my shoulders relax.

Going back around the castle took longer than I remembered. With every step, the thought that I had been tricked and would also be imprisoned grew larger and louder in my mind. I wanted to be calm, to be quiet, but everything whirled and roared just as much inside as it did outside. It was as if the darkness had found its way in and would not stop its storming.

When I came to the gate, it opened for me, and the princess stood on the other side, her skin pale as death next to the dark walls. I went inside before handing her the apple, so that she couldn't close it without letting me in. After a careful scan of our surroundings, she took the apple and pulled me through the castle. The corridors and rooms passed us by as if they were what moved and we were standing still, their conformations appearing to shift, to writhe as we passed.

The princess —I remembered that the Swede had called her Ýrr— propelled me into a bedchamber. On the bed lay a man, but his back was to me.

"I'll come back when your time is over," said Yrr, smirking at me before she closed the door behind her. I went up to the bed.

"Finnr?" The man didn't stir. I walked around to the other side and my stomach flopped at the sight of his childlike face, the memory of when I'd last seen it and why coming to vivid life in my mind. "Finnr?"

I went to the door and pressed my ear against it to listen for Ýrr, or anyone else who might be nearby. There was only silence. I bent down to peer through the gap beneath the door, and saw only an empty corridor.

I went back to the bed to shake Finnr.

"Finnr, Finnr! Wake up!" He didn't stir. What had Ýrr called him? "Galdur? Will you listen to me with that name?" No, he didn't. I shook him again, harder, but he didn't even so much as breathe differently. "Finnr! Wake up! It's me, Dagný. I've come to rescue you, like I said I would."

Still nothing.

God, what do I do? I prayed, tears coming to my eyes.

"Finnr, wake up! *Wake up!*" I shook him so roughly that he nearly fell off the bed but it did nothing. The tears spilled out into my voice and I started to weep. "Finnr, you idiot, I came all the way to the land of the dead to save you and all you're going to do is sleep? I can't carry you out of here; you're too heavy. *Finnr, wake up!*" But he wouldn't wake, no matter how hard I tried. When Ýrr came back, she found me holding Finnr and sobbing.

"Get. Out." Her eyes were weapons of hatred. Without even waiting for me to move, she pulled me off Finnr, dragged me through the castle, and pushed me out the gate. It closed behind me with a sharp thud.

I had to try again.

Quickly as I could manage without appearing too eager, I headed back to the castle windows and stood directly beneath them. I still had the golden carding comb and loom with me, and I debated which to pull out first. The apple had been enough the first time, but would Ýrr demand more for a second visit? As my hand fell on the comb, an unusual sense of peace filled my heart, relaxing my chest so completely I half wondered if my insides had turned to liquid. No, not liquid. They had fallen into the kind of sleep a child does when they know they are safe. If just the comb wasn't enough, I could always pull out the loom after.

It felt silly, fiddling with a carding comb when I had nothing to do with it, but I kept it out and made sure it would be visible from the castle window. Every moment stretched with waiting.

"Now, *that* is a fine toy," Ýrr said, leaning against the window frame. "How much do you want for it?" It was as if all her anger had evaporated. I dared not speculate as to what that might mean.

"It's not for sale, for gold or money."

"Oh, of course not." She giggled. "What else would you accept as payment?"

"I would accept permission to visit your betrothed for a time." I could barely breathe for fear that my request might be denied.

"That again? Well, at least you're simple. Yes, we can manage that again, just give me a little time before going to the gate." She withdrew from the window.

Unable to wait, I headed to the gate and stood by it for what felt like years. I went inside the moment Yrr opened the gate and handed her the carding comb. She raised an eyebrow, but led me again through to Finnr's room. As we passed through the castle corridors, I noticed tapestries, furnishings, and facsimiles of fine things, all made from darkness, all utterly empty. If this was a castle, and Ýrr and Erlendsína were supposed to be royalty, then where were the people? Where were the servants, guards, members of the court? Should I at least have been able to hear them? With their power, the two of them could have everything, and yet I could see only nothing.

Ýrr shoved me through the door to Finnr's room. "I'll get you when your time is up." The door closed almost before she had finished her sentence.

Finnr.

He lay on the bed. Still, silent. Asleep. But this time he would wake. I would wake him.

Gentle as a summer breeze, I knelt by him and whispered into his ear.

"Finnr. Galdur." Nothing. Not again. I pressed my forehead against his, willing him to wake. "Finnr, please, I know you can hear me." No, I didn't. "Wake up."

I stood and walked away, absently looking for something I could throw.

"Why, God? Why would you lead me here to him, only to come to this? Why would you encourage me, give to me, and guide me, only to bring me to failure? Tell me!" I didn't even wait for a response. I remembered what he had done out in the hills after Kaj's funeral. What he hadn't done. "You're cruel, you know that? You tell me that I'll succeed, and lead me through all this, doing things that no one else could have done, and then… then you abandon me again. How could I ever trust you?" The words flew out of me, sharp as the teeth of a predator. I hated them. This was God I was abusing, the one who made everything, who sent his son. As Father Símon would say, "a profounder embodiment of love, no one has found." I was supposed to love him… so why were these the only words my heart could say to him?

Back against the wall, I slid down to sit with my arms wrapped around my legs. If I couldn't wake Finnr now, I would have to choose between seeing him again, or saving the prisoners. I didn't want to chose. I didn't want to do anything. I wanted God or someone to come in and take over and fix everything. But he wasn't. And I didn't know what to do.

Ýrr returned with an expression of sickening victory to lead me from the room and I followed as meekly as a lamb. When the gate shut behind me, I wandered almost as aimlessly as a shade back to the place with the barred window.

"Hey, Icelandic girl!" called the Swede. "Did you find a way in?"

I sat down in the gravel. He stared at me with concerned eyes, but waited for me to speak.

"I went in twice. Twice to see the man I came here for, and he was asleep both times, so deeply that I couldn't wake him. I light one candle…" My throat closed and I had to swallow several times before I was able to speak again. "I have one more chance to go in, and I want to help you all, very much, but I came here

99

to right a wrong I'd committed, and now I don't think I'll be able to do that without doing wrong against you."

The Swede nodded, then turned to talk with the other prisoners. I simply sat, miserable, as they argued. It wasn't until the Swede poked at me through the bars that I realized they had finished.

"Go save the one you came for. If you came here once, I'm certain you can return, and with help, if needed. Perhaps you and he could even free us once he's out, or as you get him out. Just-just promise me one thing."

"What is that?"

Tears shimmered in the Swede's eyes. He blinked a few times to clear them.

"Don't forget about us."

His words echoed in my mind and heart as I returned to the back of the castle. Somehow, they had pricked a soft place, and I had to hold back tears, especially when I'd seen his face twist after saying them. I'd told him that I wouldn't forget.

When I arrived, I took out the tiny golden loom. It shone, even despite the darkness that rubbed against it, its every surface and detail exquisite with light. For a moment, I even forgot that I was in the land of the dead.

"What's that?" Ýrr was squinting at me from her window.

"A loom."

"A very tiny loom… and it looks perfect in every detail." She rested her chin on one fist. "I want it. What will you give it to me for?" Her voice held a note of greed I hadn't heard in it before, and that made me uncomfortable. Still, I kept to my lines.

"It's not for sale—"

"I *know* that, imbecile." I bristled at the word, though I did my best to keep it hidden. "Do you want to see my darling Galdur again?"

"Yes."

"Well, then, give me a moment. I'll come to the gate." I didn't wait; I knew it would make me sick with nerves. I headed straight to the front of the castle.

God, please. Please let him be awake this time. This is my last chance. I'm sorry I yelled at you before.

Again into the castle.

Again to the room.

My hands shook, fingertips cold with anticipation. Ýrr pushed me through the door, closing it with a thud. Before me, Finnr lay on the bed as he had before. My heart wanted to sink into darkness, but I held it fast. He was awake. *Oh, God, he has to be awake.*

When I came next to the bed, Finnr stirred. My hand flew to my chest. He turned over. Sat up. Smiled.

"It's good to see you again, Dagný." The sound of his voice pierced through to the hidden places in my heart, and a flood threatened to pour out of them in response. It took all my effort to hold the tears in check. I couldn't even speak.

Oh, but I knew I had to.

I told you it would work, God said, the quiet water of his words melting away the rocks in my soul. *I promised. And I keep my promises.*

"Finnr… I thought… I…" my face became tight against the

onslaught of my heart. "I thought I'd never see you again. I was afraid; so afraid. But you're here, and you're awake."

He didn't speak. He just held me while I cried like a baby. When I became calm again, we parted and he said:

"I'm so sorry I caused you pain! Ýrr had brought me here from the prison and had given me a sleeping potion both times. I'd let her because I hadn't thought, not even in my most hopeful of dreams, that you would have come for me. But when the other prisoners realized who I was and told me that you had come, I could hardly contain my joy. When Ýrr gave me the potion this time, I only pretended to drink it, my mind whirling the whole time. God had told me you would come, but I couldn't believe him. How could anyone living get to the land of the dead alone, even if they knew it was their destination?" They had told him about me? *Oh, God, thank you.*

"I wasn't alone," I said softly. "God showed me the way."

Finnr nodded. "And now that you're here, we have a chance."

"How? I can't think of any way to get both you and the other prisoners out, and I promised that I wouldn't forget about them."

"There's a way to free everyone imprisoned here, but I don't want to say it in case we're being overheard." He paused, brow wrinkled in thought. "Come to the wedding. The gates will be open, so you'll be able to get in, and we will leave this place from there."

I hoped he was right.

CHAPTER FIFTEEN:
Christian Men

I stayed close enough to the gates so that I could hear when they opened, and far enough so that I wouldn't be noticed among the shades. I tried to speed the passing of time by reciting all the writings I had memorized until my throat was nearly hoarse.

When the gate opened, the sharp creak made me jump. I entered the castle, following the shades that had started pouring in, uncharacteristically united in their direction.

We came to a large room with a low stage at one end, on which stood Finnr, Erlendsína, and Ýrr. In front of it, among the milling shades, stood prisoners, chained to the ground. I kept to the back, but I made sure that Finnr could see me.

The whole situation was bizarre. Both Ýrr and Erlendsína wore threadbare grave clothes; there wasn't a priest in sight. And then there was the presence of only shades and the prisoners among the audience. Was it simply because there were no other residents of the land of the dead, or did it serve some sort of purpose?

The shades became more or less still as Erlendsína came forwards and started to speak. Finnr quickly interrupted her.

"Before this wedding can begin, there is a test I must perform.

If I am to marry, the woman must pass it in order to prove her worthiness."

"Really?" Erlendsína sounded amused.

Finnr ignored her and picked up a shirt with three drops of tallow blackening its front. My heart ached to see those spots. "The woman who can clean this shirt is the one I will leave this land with."

Whether that was true or not, Erlendsína sniggered and whispered something to Finnr that made his whole body tense and his face turn white.

"Let's have this little ritual, then," she said in her full voice. Ýrr stepped forwards, having produced a bucket full of soapy water from the air. Finnr handed her the shirt and she began to scrub. I wished I could rush up to Finnr and pull him away. This test couldn't possibly be his plan. If she used any of her unholy magic, it would only be moments before she pulled out the shirt, clean as untouched snow.

Except, when she *did* pull it out, the shirt was worse. The tallow spots had grown and blackened, like the smearing of soot. Looking confused, Ýrr turned to her mother for help.

"You're worth none of the effort I put into having you if you can't even do a simple thing like this," snarled Erlendsína, pushing Ýrr out of the way so that she could scrub the shirt herself. But she could do no better. Furious, she immersed the shirt in the water again and pounded at it, but the fabric only became blacker and blacker with the abuse. Finnr laughed. She glared at him.

"It looks like neither of you is worth much. I bet that girl," he waved his hand in my direction, "could clean even all of this mess out." Erlendsína's glare turned to calculation the moment she saw me. She stood, back perfectly straight.

"Well, then," she said to me, "come up and show us your handiwork."

It took all of my effort to approach and climb the stage without shaking or looking at Finnr. If these two draugar with all their power could not do this, then how did he expect me to? I wanted to stop and scream at him. What kind of plan was this? Instead, eyes away from his face, I went to the bucket. And the shirt.

"Hello, Dagný," whispered Erlendsína as I walked by. The muscles in my neck and shoulders tightened at the sound of my name from that monster's lips. "I told you that you'd see my end with different eyes." I stopped, stomach twisting, and stared at her. The draugur back home had told me that, not her. Unless... She smiled, chuckling dryly. "Silly girl. When you fail, I will destroy your family, and they will curse you for it."

Please let her words be nothing but lies, I prayed, steeling myself. Then, fists clenched, I knelt next to the bucket and reached in to wash the shirt.

Dagný, careful. At first, I wasn't certain if God had really spoken, so I stopped to listen, and he said it again. *Dagný, be careful.*

Why?

They both tried to make this shirt clean. They both worked and worked to erase the past, but neither of them could, no matter their power. If you try the same, you will also fail in the same way.

My hand hovering over the shirt, I looked to the audience. Somehow, the prisoners had grown to a multitude, all in chains, all wearing the faces of people I knew like a veil of light over their own. The Swede and the others with him became my father, Auðun, Father Símon. My father's friends. In the crowd, I saw Mother, Eir, and the rest of my family. Everyone I'd ever known and some I didn't know yet somehow stood before me... and also didn't stand before me. I didn't know what it meant, and that frightened me. I looked to Finnr for some sort of assurance, but my breath grew thick when I saw Kaj's face.

God, what do I do? I dared not look back at Erlendsína or Ýrr. If everyone I had ever known was accounted for, I did not want to know whose face might be seen on those two. Erlendsína's words to me echoed through my ears with a ringing strength; I could not keep them out. God's voice came gentle in my ears, a soft breeze, a quiet stream:

'Who has believed our message, and to whom has the arm of the Lord been revealed?' A passage in Jesaja. I closed my eyes and recited with the voice of my heart, aware of his listening ears, listening myself for the moments he recited with me.

'He was despised and rejected by mankind, a man of suffering, and familiar with pain.'

'Surely he took up our pain and bore our suffering... the punishment that brought us peace was upon him.'

"This girl of yours seems to be something of an idiot," said Erlendsína, breaking through into my thoughts with assumed triumph. It shook me, but her voice could not stop my litany.

'... no weapon forged against you will prevail, and you will refute

every tongue that accuses you. This is the heritage of the servants of the Lord, and this is their vindication from me.' So I declare. So it is. Do you believe it? All the fear had fled in the face of God's presence.

"Yes." I didn't care who heard me. They could interpret my words however they wanted; I knew to whom I spoke. "Yes, because I'm a bit of an idiot and yet you keep talking to me." I could almost see God's grin. *So, what do I do?*

Absolutely nothing. Just pick up the shirt out of the water. I will do the rest. I promise. Let me right your wrong. Let me take your suffering.

How am I supposed to both do nothing and pick up the shirt?

Well, they can't see what I've done if the shirt's still in the bucket, now can they? It was my turn to grin. It made no logical sense, while in the land of the dead with the fate of not only myself but everyone I had ever known hanging on this one act, to feel as peaceful as God's words had left me. It made no sense to do nothing more than show what God may or may not do. But I had travelled here on the back of the north wind, after a journey guided by God himself, and God had made sure I would see Finnr once I'd arrived. All the things he had done filled my mind like pieces of evidence building a case for his integrity.

I picked up the shirt.

As the water streamed down from it, the fabric shed its blackness. The tallow fell away, disappearing like forgotten past. All the water left was a white shirt, spotless, still damp, but clean.

Erlendsína hissed and came towards me, hands outstretched and fingers rigid in grotesque configurations. I fell back, dropping the shirt, but then she froze and it was as if the entire land had taken a breath.

Then.

Then.

The draugs face sprang open with cracks. I stepped away, finding that she, Ýrr, and the whole castle also snaked with weakness. The cracks widened, opening as if the draugar and castle were made of bricks with too little mortar between them, opening as if something were trying to come free. Pillars of light broke through, crumbling the pieces into dust and the ground shook with a sound like thunder. I closed my eyes to keep from being blinded, but God whispered to me, and my mind put words to his voice in my heart:

No, Dagný. Keep them open. They have been shut for so long... let them see.

The light blasted through the walls of the castle, leaving no trace of it behind, not even rubble. For a moment, I could almost believe it had never been, so complete was its destruction.

The pillars coalesced into a cross twice my height, standing where Erlendsína and Ýrr had been. The audience of prisoners stared at their wrists and ankles, now free of chains, and then at the light before them. Finnr and I glanced at each other, smiling like fools. I wondered if God had said something to him, too.

Erlendsína's words to me may have been true. It may be that I was dead, and that passing through the cross meant I would be leaving my family to grieve. I didn't care. She had been wrong about my failure.

Finnr and I stepped through the cross together.

CHAPTER SIXTEEN:

Brought to Life

With a groan, I opened my eyelids. It felt as if they wanted to keep me from seeing, as if they and the rest of my body were heavier than normal. Light shone at me. I shaded my eyes with my hand and winced.

"Dagný?" It sounded like someone I knew. I tried to speak, but my throat was dry, as if made of wool. My first attempt was nothing more than a croak. "Dagný? Are you awake?"

"Finnr?" The name came hoarse from my lips.

"No, it's your mother."

"Mamma?" The light dimmed, and my mother's face became clear. She had leaned over me to block it. "Where am I?" A drop of liquid fell onto my forehead. Mother was crying. "What's wrong?"

"There's nothing wrong. Not now. You're alive."

"I thought I always was," I said as I sat up and looked around. My mother knelt beside me on short grass, green stains on her skirt from kneeling. Above her, the sun shone from the sky's zenith, wreathed in delicate clouds. I put my hand down and something hard and rough pressed into it. I picked the thing up, only to see that it was a fragment of a brick. It had lain at the edge of a pile of bricks strewn beside the broken seal of a grave-door.

"Where's Finnr?" I asked.

"The polar bear?"

"He wasn't really a polar bear —that was a curse. He's a man. Finnr!"

Dagný, look around.

I tried to stand, but Mother put a hand on my shoulder, keeping me down.

"Dagný, he's not here," she said. "He's not with you. Your body's been lying here for four days, after a storm blew in from the north. You were dead. We tried to bring you to the church for burial, but you were so heavy that we couldn't move you. Everyone was afraid that you'd become a draugur, that Finnr was a demon instead of an angel and that he'd saved us at the expense of your soul. Everyone but me." She took a breath. I barely heard her words. My thoughts were only of finding Finnr.

"Mamma, we can talk about this later. Right now, I need to find Finnr. Do you have any idea where he might be? Did you see him?" I craned my neck to look as far as I could while still on my back.

"No, we can't talk about this later."

"Mamma—"

"Listen to me! I've had to wait by your body for four days wondering if you'd rise as a monster and knowing that it would be my fault if you did. Do you have any idea of the agony I've been through?" She stared at me with wild, tear-stained eyes. I only now noticed the runnels of salt along her cheeks.

"Yes," I said, my voice soft. "Yes, I do. But it's not your fault."

"It's not? I gave you the candle. I told you to light it. That bear is an angel, like your father said, but I could only see the demon." Mother bowed her head.

I sat up, pulled her to me and kissed her on the cheek. It tasted of dried tears and self-hate.

"It's not your fault, Mamma. I took the candle. I lit it. But God brought me back, brought me here, as I am, alive. And I don't think it matters to him how we sin, only that he has healed it." I didn't know where the words came from. They came so easily, so freely, and it didn't matter that I didn't quite know if they had come from my own mind or through me from another. They were true.

They were true.

They were true.

As my mother wept into my neck, I felt a burden lift from my heart, broken loose by those words and set to fly so far away that I would not even remember it anymore.

Dagný, look around.

I already have. There's nothing to see.

There's everything to see. Mother sniffed and pulled away. She seemed to be about to stand up, but something caught her eye. Captured it. Her face turned completely white.

"Dagný, look around." An exhalation warmed the back of my head. Quickly, I turned around. Behind me stood a polar bear.

"Finnr!" I stood and wrapped my arms around his neck.

"Hello Dagný," he said, his voice rumbling through me in evident pleasure. "There's one more thing we need to do before this is all over. Come into the barrow with me." Without hesitation, I started after him. Before we entered the grave-door, Mother grabbed my hand.

"I love you." She smiled. "And I'll let the family know you're back." Behind me, Finnr broke away the rest of the bricks so that he could fit through the entrance. The sound of clay crumbling to dust… I will never forget that sound.

We went into the barrow. The smell of rot assaulted me even before we came to stand next to… the body. I didn't want to say the first thing on my mind, so I looked away from the shriveled corpse and said the second instead.

"Finnr," I said, my arms wrapped around my body as meagre protection against the dark and the stench. "Why aren't you human again?"

"I told you at the beginning," he said. "I am only called Finnr. And that witch called me Galdur. I wanted to tell you my name, but I couldn't. At that time, you saw through a glass, darkly. But now the darkness has lost its power and it is time for you to see clearly. Do you remember that night by the fire when I helped you let go of the cold you'd been holding in your bones?" I nodded. He sat on his haunches. "Sit down. Relax." I looked at the dirt, at the damp. At my brother's body. The sight of his decomposing features filled me with nausea. I pleaded with Finnr with my eyes. He only huffed and lay down.

I sat. Finnr remained silent, as it waiting for something. Wondering what he expected to happen next, I waited as well. Slowly, the smell of my brother's corpse faded, and I let my tension go with it.

"Now," said Finnr, "close your eyes and picture yourself out on the hills. God is standing in front of you, holding a book full of beautiful pictures. He opens it and begins to read…"

Once, there was a girl whose brother had died.

Was I only imagining this? I could see, inside of me, the hills outside the farm and the cloud-raked sky above them. God stood atop one hill, facing me, and I stood atop another, facing him. In his arms he held a red book with gold embossed in intricate designs on its covers. He opened the book and began to read.

She came out to the hills with me and cried out for my presence, so I told her:

His voice reverberated through the air. I could feel it touch my bones and fill them with warmth. My eyes remained closed. I remained sitting in the barrow made for my brother. But God was speaking, and I didn't know what he would say next.

"I am coming, I am coming, I am coming."

No, he hadn't.

She told me to heal her grief, so I told her:

Had he?

"I am working, I am working, I am working."

The repetition sounded like the turning of a wheel; like the pounding of water against stone. I had no doubt that he had said this. How had I not heard?

I sent her my servant, and I told her:

"Do not be afraid!" But she ran away, and the terror came to her family.

I had heard him, I realized, that wheel in the silence. I had just refused to listen.

113

When my servant could travel once again, I sent him with haste to end the terror, to bring my beloved daughter rest and healing.

My servant bore a curse from the grave, which limited his strength. He could only bless the girl and her family by taking her from that place to another, where the girl had to endure his presence in her bed every night without knowing who she slept with.

He opened to a picture of me on the bed with Finnr, lighting the candle.

Out of fear, the girl played into the hands of the curse-caster. I knew she would, and had spent a long time preparing the path she would have to take to peel the layers of fear from her heart and arrive at the hurt that I alone could heal.

He flipped through the pages, almost too fast for me to see them, and they melded together into one tapestry. Björg, asleep in her bed as God whispered dreams into her ear. Her friend, listening to me with one ear while she drank her milk, and God with the other. God himself, disguised as a fair-haired girl, sitting on a fence at a fork in the road.

That was you? I asked. He shrugged.

If I had come any other way, at any time before, you would have rejected me and my words. As it was, you listened, and believed, and I took you to your destination before East Wind left for the day.

All the winds, at home in time for my arrival. North Wind sitting on the grass, waiting for the one God had shown him was coming. God returned to the words in the book.

The girl could have turned and gone home when she heard about the land of the dead. Fear had crept around her and tried to swallow her, but she did not fall. She had heard my voice in the wind, even

114

when I had brought her to the hills after that terrible funeral, and went to the land without wind. And, in that land, she found me again.

He closed the book.

Dagný, do you know why I did all of this for you?

I shook my head.

This was never about barrows, or curses, or polar bears. He stepped across the crevasse between our hills and wrapped me in his warm arms. *Do you trust me?*

Everything that I was spoke in response: *Yes.*

Tell Kaj to wake up.

The vision broke, leaving me sitting next to Finnr in the barrow of my dead brother. I stood, eyes still closed, and steadied myself against Finnr's flank. All the times in the Bible anyone had commanded another to wake up flooded through my mind as I realized what God was telling me to do. What he was telling me I *could* do. An emotion had reached up into my throat, trying to close it, but I knew it for what it was.

Fear, I thought, and removed my hand from Finnr, *I send you away in the name of the living God.* I exhaled.

"Are you afraid?" asked Finnr suddenly.

"No, I'm not." It had lifted from me like a blanket of darkness, dissolved from my heart like a rock turning to water. To wind.

I straightened, stood apart from Finnr, eyes still closed. His warmth filled the air between us.

"Kaj—" my voice cracked. I took a deep breath, letting the peace that had come in the wake of fear settle in more deeply.

God, back then in the hills, I know now that I'd been too afraid to listen to what you really had to say. I didn't want to stop hating you.

Don't worry about it, Dagný. I already forgave you.

And I trusted him. I really did. With that, I relaxed into words.

"Kaj, wake up." Finnr sighed, the release of a thousand sorrows. His warmth gathered itself and poured around me like an unseen river until it had passed.

"Dagný?" A child's voice, followed by the sound of someone sitting up, then standing.

I opened my eyes. In the barrow with me was only my brother, looking ridiculous in his funeral clothes and healthier than he had ever been. Kaj.

Alive.

Acknowledgements

Thank you so much to Taryn for refraining from saying anything about the horrifically apparent of sleep deprivation found in the first draft, simply because I hadn't asked for feedback yet, and for your trust that I would find and fix it all when editing. If that were me, such an act would have taken massive amounts of self-control. You are fantastic.

My editor, Ruth Ellen Parlour. This book has been made much better by your help. You have a knack for finding words I'd given up on remembering. I'm sure an angel choir started singing every time I came across that in your edits.

To my mom for giving me space to edit even though it was probably frustrating that I kept taking up half the living room table. Or the sewing room, if the living room was otherwise occupied.

Thank you to everyone at the University Bible Fellowship for encouraging me, for listening to me reading the first two chapters out loud after Bible study, and for always being so ready to help when you see a need. My life has been made beautiful by your presence in it.

To everyone in the Puttytribe, you've been wonderful in your help and positivity. Thank you.

Thank you to everyone who gave me feedback on the illustrations and new cover. I've been anxious, so there's been a lot of you, and you have all helped me so, so much.

And last, but never least, to all the supporters of my Indiegogo campaign: *Thank you so much!* I wish there was a way to show you just how much I appreciate your help. Italics don't cut it. Not one bit. You are all absolutely fabulous.

About the Author

Thea van Diepen hails from the snowy land of Canada and that fairest of cities, Edmonton, Alberta. She is, of course, completely unbiased (being a psychology student) and is obsessed with Orphan Black, the books of Madeleine L'Engle, and the inner workings of the mind.

When Thea was eight years old, she took a test in school that required her to write a story. This excited her greatly, and she decided to write an epic fantasy adventure. Upon opening the test, she discovered she had to incorporate a girl going on a hike with her family. Thinking fast, she opened the story with said hike, dropped the girl into a magical world, ditching the family on the mountainside, and happily wrote whatever she wanted until the end of the test. She got honours that year.

Her website is expectedaberrations.com, home of all things that lie on the edge of the bell curve, and she can be contacted via that site, in English or French. If you *do* email her in French, please don't ask her to count in it, as she tends to skip numbers ending in six entirely by accident.

All for the Want
of
Chai

West Wind could smell the chai in the breeze before he saw the house. His house. His chai. Sitting in *his* cup while East Wind slurped it in large, self-satisfied gulps. He had told his brother not to touch the chai. He'd used those exact words.

Oh.

Damn.

Faster, ever faster, West flew, skimming the tops of mountains, rocketing towards home and —oh, not the lawn!— slowing just in time not to leave skid marks.

"East!"

"Whaaat?" East poked his head out the front door. "Can't a fellow drink his tea in peace?" He flourished a cup. West's nostrils flared.

"I told you you couldn't have my chai."

"You told me I couldn't *touch* your chai." East slurped, his eyes slits of pleasure.

"It's my tea, and you are not to have it! Not at all!"

"Oh, grow up," said East. He retreated into West's house.

Grow up? West thought, the wind of his body darkly swirling.

Grow up? You're the youngest! He slammed the door open, then winced in apology for such rough treatment.

East squatted by the fire, five or six plates in a haphazard pile next to him, empty save for crumbs. An entire fish skeleton had just fallen to the floor.

"East!" West tried to say, but his throat had strained such that all that came out was an angry squeak.

With a swig, East downed the last of his chai.

"Sure is cozy in here, isn't it?" He winked at West, then sent a spurt of wind to close the door. "Let's keep it that way."

"You have abused my hospitality for the last time, East."

"Oh, pish." East stood and clapped a hand on his brother's shoulder. "Your hospitality is as vigorous as ever. In fact, you were just about to invite me to stay for supper."

"East, if you do not leave my house right now, I will be forced to storm you out of it."

They stared at each other for a moment, West's agitation beginning to eddy the air around him. East gave West's shoulder two pats, then left.

West took a breath and let his body calm and lighten. Then he picked up the plates —after placing the fish on top— and carried them over to the kitchen, bracing himself for the inevitable chaos. He stepped over the threshold and…

"My God."

The room was spotless. Shining, almost. And, sitting on the small wooden table were two plates of carefully arranged sushi, each accompanied by a steaming mug of chai tea, a bowl of baklava between them. There was a note.

Dear brother West,

Since you have kicked me out, I suppose you will have to enjoy this wonderful food all by yourself.

Alone.

Without me.

Must be quiet.

Ah, well, I thought I'd be brotherly for a change, but it seems you caught me in the act of taking a break before cleaning the last of this up. I suppose I deserve it, being the dashing rogue that I am. Bon appétit!

Sincerely,

East

P.S. Sorry about the chai; I'll admit that giving in to its temptation made this note necessary.

P.P.S. Please let me back in. I have made you brownies.

P.P.P.S. Also, you may have sent me out before I could return your cup.

The Undead Fairy Tales Collection

Cinderella and Zombies by Emily Casey
Snow White and Zombies by Emily Casey

Forthcoming: *Revenant: Arthur* by Robert D. Marion

Also by Thea van Diepen

Dreaming of Her and Other Stories

(All titles are currently only available through the Amazon Kindle Store)

Made in the USA
Charleston, SC
22 March 2015